The Chandler Apartments

The Chandler Apartments

A Novel

Owen Hill

CREATIVE ARTS BOOK COMPANY
Berkeley • California

The Chandler Apartments is published by Donald S. Ellis
and distributed by Creative Arts Book Company

For information contact:
Creative Arts Book Company
833 Bancroft Way
Berkeley, California 94710
1-800-848-7789

Acknowledgments

Thanks to Dan Liebowitz, first reader of this book; to Ray Davis
for suggesting the title; and to Gloria Frym for helping me
find a publisher.

Thanks also to the owners, manager, and tenants of the
Chandler Apartments.

And, as ever, to Carol Jameson.

Edward Dorn and Harold Norse are quoted with permission,
thanks to Jennifer Dorn and Harold Norse.

Library of Congress Cataloging-in-Publication Data

Hill, Owen.
  The Chandler apartments / Owen Hill.
    p. cm.
  ISBN 0-88739-430-2 (alk. paper)
  1. Berkeley (Calif.)—Fiction. 2. Apartment houses—Fiction. 3. Poets—Fiction. I. Title.

PS3608.I437 C48 2002
813'.6--dc21

                                                    2002017474

Printed in the United States of America

for the poets

The Chandler Apartments

1.

    Once I had a wife, and she liked cute little cars. A little out of character for her (she was the solid career type), but charming. She looked great in convertibles, so we bought one even though Berkeley is usually a little too cool for them. Paid cash, thanks to my uncle Deke, who died with a savings account and no heirs. When we parted she bought herself a vintage Triumph, found (I swear) a Brit boyfriend, and made no claim on the Miata.

    It's a dumb car, especially for me. I'm a book scout. That is, I go to estate sales, postal auctions, the homes of the widows of college profs, the Goodwill, any place where there might be a sellable book. Then I take said books to various booksellers, starting with rare book dealers and quality used bookstores, then down the line of dusty little shops, internet sellers, and finally a dealer from Manila who sends anything in English to . . . who knows where.

    My silly little Miata (bright red . . . God help me) does impose a certain amount of self-discipline, which is a good thing for any book hound. I can only fit six or seven shopping bags (bags, not boxes—easier to handle) per haul, so I go for the cream. If I score on a bigger library, I have to prevail upon Marvin and his old Econoline, which means making him dinner, anything he likes. He likes expensive.

When we got the Meltzer library (well, not the whole thing, Moe's Books got there first) he wanted Chilean Sea bass ($17.99 a pound) and two bottles of Sattui Chardonnay. Throw in several Negronis and a few shots of Laphroig, and I could have gone to Beakins. Marv looks like an old hippie, but his tastes are yuppie all the way.

I have no off-street parking, so the Miata takes a beating. Telegraph Avenue, world famous open-air asylum, is hell on parked cars. If you can find a space at all. Often I park in another neighborhood and walk in. I moved to the neighborhood after the breakup, six years ago. The Chandler Apartments. A beautifully restored 20's building overlooking a sea of kooks. Its denizens are split down the middle, half rich kid students and half rent control survivors. I pay the rent-board-dictated price of $453.35 a month for a large, airy studio on the fourth floor. Four big windows with a view of Oakland and the hills. The grad student down the hall pays $809.94. The owner, a New York/Berkeley lefty, is surprisingly nice about the situation. For the first couple of years the noise from Telegraph drove me nuts, but now I find it comforting. Call it a sense of community. Even the craziest street person knows my face, and for a few quarters a month they treat me as a friend. There's a sense of adventure, of movement, on the Avenue. That's a scarce commodity in late capitalist California (America? the industrialized world?). The bongos, the Krishnas, the cries of imaginary friends have stopped disturbing me now. Actually, they drive all thoughts of loneliness from my mind. Though I've never been especially prone to loneliness.

Scouting isn't making me rich. Actually, if it weren't for cheap rent the wolf would be camping on the front stoop. Old Uncle Deke helps a little. Just under $20,000, now in a

CD. Mad money. And an occasional adventure takes me out of the state, or the country. Last splurge was a trip to Paris with an old friend, recently released from an ugly relationship. She needed to do something dramatic, and I was handy. I guess I have a knight in shining armor complex. Well, no guessing about it. Kind of embarrassing in pre-post-feminist Berkeley. It gets me into scrapes, but I enjoy playing good Samaritan, especially to a certain type of person, lithe and flip, with underlying vulnerability and a great kiss. Maybe I'm a cad. After the Paris trip the Miata got keyed, and when I innocently asked her ex about the wound, I had to duck a wild flail, kick him in the knee, and beat it back to the Chandler. I'm too small (5'8", 142) to win most fair fights, so I've learned how to hit and run.

2.

Peggy Denby is, like me, a small press poet. That is, we write poetry with no hope of being published by a major house. My books have been published by the likes of Angry Dog Press and Thumbscrew Press, and in mags like *Gas, Bluebook*, and *Twatsdelight*, which is Peggy's. *Twat* is best described as irreverent post-post-punk-pseudo cute. You know the look. Fake leopardskin and kitty glasses. The *Twatsdelight* logo features a martini glass. And that is Peggy's look, too.

Her message had said "Meet me at that place where you always go," and I dutifully entered the Drunken Boat at the right time, scoring an outside table under a tree on a beautiful May Monday afternoon. Drunken Boat has one real waiter and a bunch of kids. Real waiter took my table so I ordered a Negroni. I didn't order for Peggy because I hadn't seen her in at least two years. Last time I ordered for someone I hadn't seen in a while it was a mistake. He'd become a twelve stepper, and I had no choice but to drink his stout for him. Sound advice: never drink a Negroni with a stout chaser.

The wise waiter brought me the perfectly chilled drink. I took a nibbling sip, tasting the bitter Campari on the tip of my tongue, the part that better detects sweet things, then I smelled for the gin, which was, thankfully, there. Then I took a slightly bigger sip, and treated the rest of my tongue to the flavors. The third sip was really more of a slug. I tried to collect my thoughts. I've had a crush on Peggy for ten years, and five years ago we had what I guess could be called an affair (we slept together more than once). Despite being intimate we were never close, really. We had some nice talks, but they were mostly about poetry or art, nothing too personal. I would have pushed it further. Like I said, I have a crush on her. But she wouldn't let it go that way. For one thing, she wanted a real husband, and I pride myself on not being a real anything. Well, I like to think I'm real, as in honest, but I can't fit the role. Any role. I can't even fit the role of the misfit, a role that may have intrigued her. I work too hard, always pay my bills, keep my (many) bad habits in check.

When Peggy married Thomas we stopped seeing each other. I still appeared in her mag, and I once featured her in my (now defunct) mag, *Blind Date*. But I think I made Thomas uncomfortable, or the both of them, or something. I saw her a couple of years ago before they went off to England for Thomas's unofficial sabbatical. He's up at

Cal, a lecturer in English Lit. Or I should say, was. He died a couple of months ago. I sent Peggy a card and kind of expected a call. It didn't come until yesterday.

She was only a few minutes late. She looked astonishingly beautiful. What is a man supposed to say when a woman loses weight? Or, to put a finer point on it, what is a man in Berkeley supposed to say? She was one of those women who could pull off being chunky, but now she wasn't chunky. She looked like an athlete. The eighties nerd look had always worked for her, I guess, but anything would work. The blonde hair was very short now, and the black glasses seemed bigger on her smaller face. Her skin didn't seem as white as before. She must be exercising outside. She kissed me full on the lips, but it wasn't a sexy kiss. Our deft waiter appeared, and she ordered straight Beefeater, ice, no lime, and after he left, said, "I'd have ordered more, but it seems weird to order a double in a garden." She was right. The Drunken Boat is more a café. I usually have my second drink at home.

"I missed you, Peggy."

"Missed you too. My life's a mess. Do you still like to give aid and comfort to lonely women?"

"I suppose it's a fault. And most of the women I know would probably do better without me."

"Don't be so modest."

Then we got off the subject for a while, talking about her new book. Experimental short stories, "kind of languagy." I tried to steer things back to her messy life, partly for the sake of gossip, but also because I sensed that she really did need help. She was slippery though, only half referring to being depressed, to having "big problems." Finally I got bored and asked her outright. "Alright, I'll tell you, but not here. Come with me back to my place."

And so we got into her Volvo, not the new kind, but one of the classic old ones that artsy women so often drive, and went to her place on Lake Merritt.

She lived on the tenth floor of a newish condo, down near Playland. The living room faced San Francisco, the kitchen looked out across the lake. The big tinted windows didn't seem to open. I thought of a hotel where I once stayed in Waikiki, my memory jogged by the Hawiiana that filled the apartment. Bobble-headed dolls and leis littered the end tables. Mylar-framed Don Ho record covers, fake flowers, funny ashtrays. I often feel confused in places like these, because I actually like this junk. My grandmother and my dear great-aunt Dinah decorated this way; it brings back nice memories. But I understand that I'm supposed to feel some sense of irony. I don't. Too much Robert Lowell, I guess. The lowest-common-denominator type is lost on me.

I sat on the futon couch, which was covered in a material that, in my surfer youth, we called "jams." Sky blue background with a white floral design. My first love wore a skirt like that. Peggy offered me drink. I opted for bubble water. The situation seemed serious. I wanted a clear head. She went into the kitchen and made us drinks. I assumed that hers was alcoholic.

"What's the problem, Peggy?"

She sat on the floor in front of the couch, a hideous driftwoody coffee table between us.

"It's still difficult to talk about anything having to do with Thomas. I'm still grieving. But something's terribly wrong. When he discovered that he was sick, he wanted to travel. He called the trip a sabbatical because he didn't want people to know. He just wasn't ready to talk about it. We thought he had at least a year. But by the time we got to Rome he was pretty sick. He insisted on taking the train down to Calabria, and then on to Sicily. I got him to a hospital in Palermo, and he got a little stronger. One day I returned to the hotel after sight-seeing to find that he'd been taken to the hospital. He was dead by the time I got there. Less than a month after the initial diagnosis.

"In Rome we stayed at the Margutta, on the Piazza Del Popolo. We went down to one of the cafes the first morning. He pulled some papers from his book bag. There was a bankbook, a regular passbook, and a couple of bank statements in envelopes. The passbook had a balance of $27,503 and change. The statements were for CD's and a mutual fund, each worth over $50,000. I was shocked that he had so much money, considering the way he spent. We always kept those things separate, and we didn't talk about it much. He made more than me, of course, but I do alright with the tech writing and various temp things. He paid three quarters of the rent and helped out on vacations. But we never talked about the specifics. He said it would be easy enough for me to get the money, even though we weren't legally married. As Thomas always said, Why bother? He'd made a will. But when he died, and it was time to straighten these things out, I found that the money wasn't there. Large chunks of the accounts had been withdrawn, every few days, and deposited into his checking account. Almost a half a mil was drawn from that account, mostly by checks made out to cash."

"Do you have a contact at the bank?"

"Yes, Dean. Dean Centro. He said that it would be easy enough to do. The checks were cashed at various banks, and there were lots of ATM withdrawals."

"But Thomas was pretty ill. How'd he do it?"

"We don't know, although he was up and around at least part of the time."

"Does his son know about this?"

"Yes, although he doesn't know the amount. He suspects that I did it. There's a daughter too, Stephanie. A spoiled little dotcommer. She also assumes that I took the money. They both hate me, the way that kids often hate young second wives. I'm thirty-one, two years older then Stephie, and three years younger than Hart. And I was to be left a larger cut, half, with the children splitting the other half. Also, I got the apartment. But I'll have to sell. I can't afford these payments."

"Have you talked to the police?"

"Yes, but there's been no crime. They aren't too interested."

"I'll talk to some people, but I'm no detective."

"I've heard that you've done some work like that."

"A little, once or twice, kind of by accident. Maybe you should call Sam Truitt. He makes a living at this sort of thing."

"Oh yeah, Sam Truitt, poet-detective. Problem is, he's teaching at Naropa this summer. To be frank, he was my first choice."

"Thanks. You could, you know, call a non-artsy detective. A pro."

"I couldn't do that. Too painful. What I really need is a friend. But, if by chance you do find some of this money, I'll give you some. Say, twenty thousand, if you recover it all?"

"I'll talk to some people. And on those other jobs I got some expense money. Just gas and lunch, and plane fare if I need it. Or you could pay this month's rent and I'll devote full time to it."

She went into the drawer of an end table and pulled out an envelope. Counted out six one hundred dollar bills.

"Do you always have that much cash on hand?"
"Drug money. They still don't take cards."

3.

Marvin is my best friend, and, in a way, my landlord. He owns the garage where I store my books. It's a small one, attached to his old bungalow-style house in North Berkeley. He bought the place in the mid-seventies, before Chez Panisse, The Cheeseboard, and Black Oak Books made the neighborhood upscale. He's "old Berkeley," meaning that his politics are to the left of Mao, but that this doesn't stop him from appreciating the better things in life: Niman Ranch beef, good wine, trips to Cuba. He drives his old van down to Silicon Valley a couple of times a week, where he makes a ton of money doing something that I'll never understand. When people ask him what he does he says, "I'm kind of a programmer. I guess." He looks and dresses like Neil Young. He refuses to tell me his age, but I'd guess he's in his late forties, about ten years older than me.

Once a week I make him dinner, rent on the garage. This week I made shrimp ravioli, and I got off cheap with a Pinot Grigio. Dinner conversation revolved around SUVs, and the types who drive them. He drives a gas-guzzling monster too, but at least his has some style. The Peggy situation didn't come up until I started serving the ricotta cake and the grappa.

"So, is this what you're doing for a living now?"

"This?"

"Helping people, mostly women. Getting expense money, and a little something after the job. It is more profitable than scouting."

"I'm not *doing* anything. There was one job, then another. Now this. Word of mouth. I won't be printing business cards. After all, I don't really know what I'm doing. I can't use a gun, can't really fight. I was never a cop."

"You're a pretty good street fighter. And, like any book bum, you're a good con-man and a good liar. But your best qualification for the job is that people don't take you seriously. You're no threat, until you kick 'em in the balls and run."

"You can write my resume.'"

"Clay Blackburn, P.I. Sounds like a TV show. That masculine name had to come in handy someday." He punctuated this remark by downing his grappa. Signaled for another.

"Also featuring Marvin Clarke, marginal character, nerdy sidekick, sometime computer whiz."

"Fuck you. Okay, so there's Peggy the widow, and some missing money. And it's worth $20,000 if you find it. Where do you go from here?"

"There's a son and a daughter. And there's Peggy. I'll start asking questions and see how it plays. And I could talk to somebody at the bank."

"I could get his records easily enough."

"Really?"

"If it's on a computer it can be found. You'll owe me some dinners though."

Deal.

4.

Marvin called the next morning, asking for Thomas's mother's maiden name, which of course I didn't have. Called back a few minutes later to say that he didn't need it, he had the info, and he'd give me the lowdown "at dinner." I hung up and the phone rang. Peggy wanted to take me to dinner. She had things to talk about. I called Marvin back, got a quick summary, and rescheduled him for the following night. I didn't want anything to get in the way of an intimate dinner with Peggy Denby.

The lowdown wasn't really low, though. Thomas had been draining the accounts of cash for months, a little at a time. He'd probably shown Peggy old statements, because by the time they hit Calabria they were pretty well drained—by check, ATM, and phone transfer to another checking account. I'd suspected that. I wondered where that money went. I figured he'd spent it on something fun, in his last months on earth. Drugs or something. Why not? Anyway, I didn't think I had much chance of recovering it. Cash doesn't stay cash for very long. I'd have dinner with her and hear her out, but the $600 and a nice dinner was the best I could hope for.

Oliveto has a place in local culinary history now, and it has upgraded along with the neighborhood. But I still remember it as friendly and unpretentious. I used to eat breakfast downstairs a lot when I lived in Rockridge. When my second chapbook came out the management let me do a reading in one corner of the café. Now the downstairs has tablecloths and service, and breakfast would be a splurge.

I waived the waitress away and wound my way through the crowded room and back to the bar. No hard liquor downstairs, which meant no Negroni. I ordered a Punt e Mes with soda. The bartender had a starched white shirt, just like Paris. She also had about fifteen pieces of jewelry pierced through various parts of her, which is probably just like Paris, too. I wanted to make conversation, but the place was too crowded. They were playing (I swear!) the Gypsy Kings on the stereo, which is just like somewhere; somewhere in Europe. To match the blotchy spongy paint job, the arched doorways, the tile floor. Euroland. I wondered if the Gypsy Kings are camp yet, and not knowing made me feel old. The bartender brought me some pistachios and two olives, compliments of the house, and accidentally (?) brushed my hand, which made me smile. I said, with a frown, "Do you like this music?"

"No, the management makes us play this bullcrap."

I liked her style. The other bartender was a taut little guy, a mystery-eth of the type that grow hereabouts. African American? Pacific Islander? Mexican? Who cares. Skin like . . . pick a nice tan thing, a light shade of wood, a cappuccino, milk chocolate. Whatever. His t-shirt was shortish, like what you'd expect a young girl to wear, but he wore it well. He bumped into my server, and she put one arm around him and giggled. I felt ancient, although I've only got about ten years on them. I'd sell my soul to watch them fuck, I was thinking, as Peggy Denby came into the café.

There's a woman who works at a certain bookstore in Santa Monica, a store that specializes in art books. Since the mid-eighties she's been wearing the same uniform to work: A very short black dress, heavy black glasses, Doc Maartens. Short blonde hair, LA beach tan. Severe facial expressions, then a slow smile. She is on my short list of reasons to live. We've never had a conversation, but I've heard her speak. She has a deep voice, like Lauren Bacall. In the fifteen years that I've "known" her she has grown more beautiful. Our relationship is, for me, the only marriage that could work. And now here's Peggy Denby, same outfit. A little gawkier than my Beatrice, perhaps. And she puts her hand on my shoulder, and leans down, and in a voice an octave lower than I remember, says, "Ready to come upstairs?" and I climb the stairs with my arm around her, hand on her hip.

Upstairs at Oliveto there's an air of excitement. The yuppies and amateur restaurant reviewers are waiting to be entertained. We get a good table, looking out at College Avenue. I have to admit that I'm excited too. Great food with a beautiful woman. Remind myself that she's recently widowed, probably not ready for anything too heavy. Try to think of something I liked about Thomas. Can't.

The appetizers are ridiculous, but they taste good. Tiny pieces of prosciutto and artichokes are strewn around a huge platter. A couple of olives. I look around at the other diners. They nibble, roll their eyes to the ceiling, sip some wine. Look down at the table, as if deciphering some ancient code. Nod their approval.

Peggy orders the wine, and it's perfect. The faux rustic

food arrives, spit-roasted meats, Swiss chard. We still haven't said much. Finally,

"There's more to all of this than I've told you."

"I figured as much, Peggy."

"Something went on in Italy. Thomas gave me the slip a few times. Lots of phone calls at the hotel. He had these sidelines."

"Sidelines?"

"Stuff. African stuff, Greek stuff."

"Peggy, I don't know if I can help you. I'm no pro. But you trusted me enough to pay me the six hundred. Why don't you just tell me what you know, think, and want. If I think I'm in over my head I'll return the money. And you know I'll be discreet. For starters, what do you mean by stuff?"

"Artifacts. He was, in his words, kind of an archeologist. He loved to travel, and he'd pick things up. After awhile he got a reputation, and people, dealers I guess, would come to him. Sometimes he'd represent collectors. He never used the term black market, but he'd buy, say, a little piece of folk art, a trinket, as he called them, and he'd leave it in the hotel room. We'd come back, and it would be gone. Then, weeks after getting home, someone would deliver it to the apartment. Then it would disappear again."

"Weren't you curious?"

"Of course. And I loved looking at the artwork. But when I asked about it all he'd make a joke, or he'd say, 'Don't worry, there's no real risk.' It didn't seem like such a big deal. After all, who, in this town, hasn't done a little smuggling? When I was twenty I lived for a summer off some hash that I bought in Amsterdam. If Thomas was buying and selling a few trinkets, no big deal."

"But now you're starting to worry?"

"Well, there's the missing money. And he did die suddenly."

"I thought he was ill."

"Yes, but he was supposed to have some time left. And I wasn't there when he was taken from the hotel. I was told that a maid discovered him and called an ambulance."

"Peggy, I can try and find the money for you, but I want no part in anything deeper. If you think somebody killed him, we'll call the cops."

"The cops would laugh. Anyway, I don't expect you to find a murderer. But I think he was into something deep, involving lots of money. More than he let on. And I'm legal heir to half of it. Well, legal is probably the wrong term. But if you help me, we could split my part."

"How much? And where might it be?"

"I don't know, but he hinted that he'd come across some 'special trinkets'. He kept using that phrase."

I didn't give her a definite answer. She ordered a half-bottle of dessert wine, then a glob of a chocolate something, then coffee. Visions of Roman statuary danced in my head, along with Fra Angelico, Da Vinci, other crazy stuff. My poet side was giving in to the romance of it all—and to Peggy, who was leaning close, talking about other things, personal stuff, old times . . . pale blue eyes can be a problem for me, and a certain type of deep voice, with a certain timbre, the right mix of breath in the vowels, can talk me into anything. Sometimes I fight it for a while, sometimes I don't, but at some point I just let go.

5.

I had visions of a sexy weekend in Hawaii world, but it didn't turn out that way. The should we-shouldn't we dance seems to be part of my karmic make-up. I just bring it out in people. She had one vodka (no mixer), her eyes glazed over, and she began thinking and feeling out loud. Life-story time. And I was drawn into it, and she heard my story, or at least the sitting-on-the-floor-with-a-woman-late-at-night version, and then we were closer friends than anticipated. The situation had some weight. I've slept with friends and I've had it be good. Actually, come to think of it, I've slept with most of my friends, although with some we really did just sleep. It's a tricky situation, which is what makes it delicious. In order to make it work you need just the right amounts of time and space. Outside interests help. They keep the focus from getting too sharp. But the key is this: an almost Zen-like lack of expectations. Being a poet, I think of it as a kind of negative capability. You dive into the sex-friendship, see where it goes, hope for the best. Let the currents carry you toward the non-shore, the non-goal. And remember to enjoy the water. Because if the thing doesn't work out (whatever work out means) you're both going to sink like bricks.

And so the voice of experience whispered, Take it slow. And I sensed that she was hearing the same voice. Wasn't always like that for me. But as the big poet said, I have had to learn the simplest things last. Which made for difficulties.

She went into the kitchen, after two A.M. I guessed, and came out with one tumbler about a quarter full of a very smooth scotch, and we shared it standing by the window, looking out at the lake and the skyline. A good kiss, then a better one. A few more. I'm tired, me too, you shouldn't drive, you shouldn't either. I'll take the couch. No, you take it. Is this OK? Yeah. But then we sat on the couch and talked some more. At some point she got up and went to bed.

Next morning she came out wearing a goofy short robe. Another Hawaiian print. Went outside and got a *Chronicle*. She started some coffee. There was nothing studied about her. She bumped into things, her hair fell into her eyes. Her robe was barely fastened, in a way that should have been coy. But I don't think she was capable of coy. You rarely meet a beautiful person, of either sex, who isn't on some level aware of their beauty, or at least of the attention they attract. Here was an exception. The great haircut just happened to be comfortable for her. She got a tan because the sun relaxed her. Exercise made her feel healthy. Vanity had little to do with these matters. I liked that a lot. Then she lit a cigarette, which surprised me.

"I didn't know you smoked."

"Once in awhile. It's nice having you here. Sorry I wasn't ready to go all the way. God, what a silly phrase. I feel like I'm in high school. Do you ever get flustered, Clay? I'm flustered. I'm probably too old to be flustered, but I am. I'm a widow, imagine. A widow."

Her voice broke.

"I'm almost always flustered. A constant state. You won't know me when you finally see me calm."

"Now? You're flustered now?"

Her voice was strong again. I had pulled her out of it.

"Of course I am. I've been attracted to you for years, and last night we got this close. Don't apologize. It's OK. It just worked out that way. But my pulse is weird, I feel fuzzy, I can't hold a thought. Flustered."

"Flustered." She smiled as if we'd invented the word. First word of our own personal language. "Clay, I lost my husband, and now I'm into some weird shit that I can't understand. This isn't my life. I write experimental verse! I'm most comfortable when I'm swimming in words. I've always pulled away from life. My heroines are Emily Dickinson and Leslie Scalapino. I don't trust my senses. My friends are mostly academics. You fascinate me, I mean the way you live. The apartment on Telegraph, digging for old books. All the nuts you hang out with. But I don't know how close I'd want to be to that."

"You came to me, dear."

"For help, because you're out in the world more."

"Don't you think you're overdoing this a little? You do live in Oakland. Look outside your window, isn't there a shooting or a drug deal happening out on the lake?"

"Just help me out, Clay."

I said I would.

And then she surprised me again, by going into the kitchen and making breakfast. "My habit has always been to cook for my lovers." Lovers?

We talked like a couple till the eggs came, and they were just plain scrambled eggs, but they were good.

This became our pattern for the next few weeks. I didn't doubt that eventually I'd move off the couch and into the bedroom. I knew the attraction went both ways. I felt a little frustrated at times, but I enjoyed her company enough to endure. When she had a reading in L.A. I was entrusted with a key. I came in twice a day for the three days and fed her cat, Gertrude Stein. I began to worry about the situation. I've been told by various people that I fear commitment. Actually, fear has nothing to do with it. I am completely (sometimes masochistically) committed to my friends, my lovers, my work, my art. I just happen to think that traditional marriage is a dismal, dreary way to live. When I was young and stupid, I shrugged, said, Try anything once! and tied the knot. Like I said, once I had a wife. Waste of time. There's one simple thing I learned early.

I wasn't entirely sure how Peggy Denby felt on the subject. Oh well, my head was still above water. Negative capability.

6.

Marvin found out about some math books in San Jose. We took the van down. The books were good. Fifteen bags of graduate texts, published in Germany. The nerd who owned them was moving to a new place in Aptos. Seems he struck it rich in some high tech way, and he just wanted to lighten his load before moving to a huge house by the sea. He took about a dollar a book. Worth at least ten apiece at Moe's.

I felt a little giddy as we loaded the Econoline. I suggested that we go to Santa Cruz and stay in a motel by the boardwalk. There's a Mexican dive restaurant I really like down there, Tampico. I had a vision of waking up, fuzzy from tequila, then clearing my head by jumping into the waves. Of course Marvin was all for it. Marvin's up for anything that can be consumed. After he agreed, I added that I'd like to swing by Natural Bridges and talk to Hart Denby. He groaned, but said OK.

We knew Hart from here and there. He was an artist, poet, lecturer, café intellectual. Dabbler. For a time he owned a bookstore in San Francisco that didn't go. Lately he'd been a sort of literary entrepreneur, booking readings and chauffeuring famous writers around. He had a show on KPFA and one on KZSC, the Santa Cruz college station. He'd bought the house by the beach when houses there were cheap. It was the kind of 70's beach box that surfers used to share. Probably worth three quarters of a mil now.

He seemed happy when I called, but he didn't invite me up to his place. We met in a bar downtown. The Red Room, or that's what everybody's called it since I lived there in the mid-seventies. It was a dive back when I was a regular. Then it became retro, and popular with students. Judging from the lack of happy hour customers, it had fallen out of favor with the cocktail generation. Hart is a good looking man with long brown hair and new-agey, too-clear grayish eyes. He announced that he was just back from Cuba, and that it was Wonderful, but also a little sad. He shook his head, didn't quite cluck his tongue. I felt Marvin tense up. Marvin goes down there a couple of times a year. His mission is to spend as much American

money as possible in a communist country. He fully sup-
ports Castro, and I suspect he's done some kind of work
for the Cuban government. I have the normal, Berkeleyite
liberal soft spot for Castro, Che and Co., but I can't support Castro's cutthroat ways. But then, I don't support
any political leader. As Marvin has pointed out, many
times, brutality is part of being a head of state, anywhere.
Marvin sees Castro as our asshole, an asshole for the
downtrodden.

Marvin sensed, and later conversation proved, that
Hart went down for cheap rum, cheap boys, cheap girls,
cheap whatever. All the things that Santa Cruz had to
offer before the earthquake. Well, subtract rum and add
cheap pot. After the town was leveled in '89 the Chamber
of Commerce types took over, and now the place looks
and feels like Santa Barbara. Another victory for the
shopping mall that took over California.

"Yes," sighed Hart, "the poverty is really sad. But
when I'm there I feel such a sense of the authentic. The
place is poor yet unspoiled. You look at the children there,
and their faces are so open!"

Marvin was gearing up for a speech. If I didn't do
something soon, he'd be banging the café table, quoting
Marx. I decided to get right to another sore point. At least
Marvin had little stake in this one.

"I've been seeing a lot of your stepmom."

"Don't call her that. Dad must have been temporarily
insane. Why are you seeing her?"

"We seem to be traveling in the same circles. Did you
know she's having trouble with the estate?"

"Of course. But the answer is simple. She took the
money, at some point, or talked him out of it. And now it's
spent and she wants more. She's getting around to blam-

ing me for it. Me or Stephie. And she's got Dean Centro on her side. That creep. I hate banker types."

Marvin was getting ready to pounce. I kicked him under the table. I pointed out that Peggy is an artist type.

"My stepmother, as you call her, is a fake. Her poetry stinks. Double bubble lingo-babble."

"Not authentic like yours, eh Hart? Plumbed from the depths of the working classes? How much did you pay your employees when you owned that crummy book-store?" This from Marvin, who was just getting started.

I couldn't afford to let him get rolling. I needed information. I listed the questions in my mind: Did Hart know how much money was involved? About his father's love of trinkets? Did he notice a change in his father's spending habits?

Sometimes fate throws one a fish. Marvin got up to go to the toilet. He asked me to order him another drink. I didn't. I had five minutes to talk to Hart. He claimed he didn't know how much was involved. He shared his father's love of collecting; they spoke about it often. But he didn't know his father's sources. I didn't buy that one. I nudged things in the direction of Thomas's spending habits, but he dummied up.

Marvin returned with a killer look in his eyes. Hart looked other-worldly. Too much time in the hot tub, I guessed. I paid the bartender, shook hands with Hart, got Marvin the hell out of there.

Tampico was a fiesta. End of semester party time. Our table was by the kitchen, but relatively quiet. Every so often we would hear a shriek coming from the direction of the bar, followed by laughter and applause. I faced a huge trophy fish, the kind that Hemingway might have caught.

This inspired me, so I ordered a seafood plate and extra tortillas. Pacificos, with shots of tequila on the side. Life is good in Santa Cruz, especially if you don't have to live there. Marvin drank his first shot in one gulp, not his usual style. He was pissed.

"That lingo-babble line is mine! I used it in a review in Poetry Flash. Rich bastard. How did he get so rich?"

"Story is that he sold his part in the store to his partner. Bought a couple of houses. Land rich, with lots of debt. A postmodern success story."

"He probably stole Peggy's money."

"How? There's no proof." I tasted my tequila. We'd ordered the high-end stuff. If the richest gold bullion could be turned into a drink it would taste like this. I decided to let the Hart subject drop. Marvin is very persuasive. I needed to keep my mind open. I couldn't make up my mind until it was time to make up my mind. I sank into myself, said, Clay, just poke around. See how it plays. There's no deadline. After all it's only money. Nobody's going to die or starve if it isn't found. And, there's this new thing with Peggy. That's the most interesting part of all of this.

Talk of politics, poetry. Relationship war stories, travel plans. Nothing having to do with the book business. That subject is off limits when we're having fun. The food was perfect. Spicy and greasy in all the right places. Marvin ordered flan, as an excuse to sit a little longer. Finally we decided to stand at the bar and have one last shot of the good stuff before heading on to the motel.

The bar was a scene. Young, beautiful amateur drinkers were talking too loudly and bumping into each other. A too-new jukebox was playing great Mexican music. Lots of accordions and horns, and high sad voices that immediately grabbed me, and dragged me down about a thousand miles to La Paz and a certain group of expats that almost ruined my life, but in a good way. I looked over at Marvin and his eyes were glazed over, no doubt reliving some adventure south of the border. He went to school in San Miguel de Allende, then hung around for a year, then spent some time in Central America doing who-knows-what for the right (left) side.

I noticed a woman at the other end of the bar. Not as young or beautiful as the students. But sexy. She was sitting, facing away from the bar, talking to a clump of coeds. They moved on, and she swung back to face the bartender and order another beer. I knew I'd seen her, but I was a little fuzzy on where. She caught my eye and came over. We were halfway into a hug before I remembered Stevie, a buyer at Logo's Books and Records. A second later I heard Marvin, almost at a yell, say "STEVIE O'HARA! How the HELL . . . ?" and I remembered that they'd had something, a fling? Or was it more serious? Couldn't remember.

People from the other California have a thick drawl. I mean people from Stockton, Salinas, Palmdale, Merced . . . anyplace but L.A. and San Francisco. Once, a twerpy little grad student at Cal confided to me that he'd had a difficult time losing his accent. He'd grown up about a hundred miles from the Bay Area. Stevie wore the accent very well. She seemed proud to be a hick. Jeans and boots, long dark auburn hair. No cowboy hat, but I remembered seeing her wearing one. She looked like a country singer, before country singers started looking Hollywood. Emmylou Harris type.

"You guys havin fun down here? You know you coulda called."

"I didn't know you still liked me." Marvin was half standing, swaying a little, wearing a goofy smile.

"Sheeyit, Marvin. I still love ya." Big smacking kiss. "You guys bring me any good books?"

I didn't want Marvin to spill the beans. She'd want those math books, but I knew I'd make more money in Berkeley. As Marvin took a breath to speak I jumped in: "No Stevie, just a pleasure trip."

She was wearing a white T-shirt with the sleeves ripped off. I was noticing this, and the dark auburn hair that fell on her shoulders, when I also noticed Hart Denby enter the bar, flanked by a couple of fratboy types. Kids like that didn't use to come to Santa Cruz. These guys looked like Nazis. How is it that you can tell the punk buzzcuts from the fascists? Must be the pleated khakis. Hart saw me and pretended not to. I think. They went to a table in the back, Hart's back to me. One of the kids came to the bar and ordered. Marvin was too excited by Stevie and the Tres Mujeres to notice much. I ordered another round and waited for Marvin to go empty his rather weak bladder.

"Hart Denby's here. Do you see him around much, Stevie?"

"Fucking bastard's sellin me books like a sonofabitch, every two or three days."

"Getting ready to move?"

"He won't say. Good stuff though. Hard to deal with. Thinks he knows more'n me about books. If he's so good, why doesn't he get back in the business?"

Hart and friends downed their drinks and beat it fast. Marvin came back, none the wiser. No bar fight tonight. I decided to excuse myself and let Marvin and Stevie catch up on each other's lives.

The sea/mountain air felt great as I walked back to the boardwalk area. I went down to the amusement park. Nothing's quite as creepy as a closed carnival. There was some phosphorous on the waves, and a full moon. Full-on spooky. The ancient roller coaster was lit by floodlights, as was the log ride, a generic amusement where tourists ride big "logs" into the "river." A little thrill in the groin, a splash of water. Not a bad idea.

The motel had a balcony that faced another balcony, but by moving all the way to the right and sitting on the railing I could see the ocean, and a little of the southern tip of Monterey Bay. I went inside, leaving the sliding door open. I got comfortable on the bed, then I took a long shower. A little thrill in the groin, a splash of water, and then to sleep.

Marvin called at four to tell me he'd be staying at Stevie's, and that he'd pick me up at the motel at check-out time. Thank you, Marvin. I got back to sleep for a couple of hours, then I was up for the day. I did a mental hang-over check and came up healthy: no migraine, not squeamish, no signs of dehydration. I felt a little regretful. Not as wild as I used to be. I went outside in a bathing suit and T-shirt. Down to the boardwalk again, then a little north to the city beach. The realtors haven't gotten around to gussying up this part of the waterfront. The tacky big hotel at the north end of the beach is an imposing reminder that humanity is eating up the world at an alarming rate. But the pier is still kind of shack-like, and the Coconut Grove, a 30's dance hall, still stands proudly. There's an interesting mix of lowlife types: punks, trailor trash, old hippies. Soon someone will decide to clean up the area. See: Santa Barbara.

It was getting light, the beginning of a very warm day. Still, I knew the water would be cold. Always is in Northern California. I felt grateful that the surf was flat. I'm only a fair swimmer. I jumped into the freeze without testing the water. A couple of crazies applauded, and I got up and bowed. It was too cold for a real swim. I got out, winded, feeling on top of the world. Hey, I'm in love, I said aloud. And I wondered if Peggy had been thinking of me.

I was back and dressed just in time for check-out. Marvin drove up, looking very bright-eyed. He had the robust, healthy look of the just-been-laid. We exchanged knowing looks.

"I don't suppose you and Stevie talked about Hart Denby."

"Actually, he was mentioned. We smoked some pot that she got from him. Seems he's still a pothead. Can't go a day without it. Grows it in his backyard. He gave her some as a semi-bribe. She still turned down most of his books."

We drove home in silence, except for Marvin's occasional humming.

7.

Sunday afternoon on the southside of Berkeley on a very warm day in late spring. There was a celebration in and around People's Park, the anniversary of some riot, in which someone was brained by a club or shot, but his/her death was not in vain as the forces of scruffiness held on to this empty lot, keeping it out of the hands of the evil board of regents. Oh well. The War of The Roses was probably a tawdry affair too. Holidays and festivals are probably the only good legacy of war. And on this glorious day South Berkeley was putting on a great, goofy party.

I waded through the park and over to Haste Street to watch the skaters. Boys in their late teens, shirts off, rolling up a ramp and falling back. Seeking that feeling in the groin. And, in the audience, little girls and lecherous old guys like me, seeking the same thing. A punk band takes the stage behind me and starts to play. They look kind of silly in the sunlight, all in black sweatshirts, but they have good sneers and the music is just bad/good enough to show that they get it. Out on the lawn a few crazies are speaking to their imaginary friends. Old hippies are dancing the same dance they've danced for thirty-five years. When the forces of boredom won for good a few losers moved from the hinterlands to The City. Then San Francisco got too expensive and they moved to Berkeley/Oakland. Something like that probably happened in parts of NYC. And Amsterdam. Any place else? If you appreciate lost causes you can fall in love with this place. Casablanca in the forties couldn't have been much more interesting and diverse. Sadly, if you listen closely that mainstream steamroller can be heard, crossing the Bay Bridge. Soon Berkeley will be a conquered province. What will become of us?

I walked down Haste Street, past Amoeba Records and the tattoo places. Thought about stopping for coffee at Café Med, but didn't. Too anxious to get home. Entered the lobby of the Chandler with a smile on my face. Through the lobby, well-preserved 1930s, with a big mirror and wallpaper, dark wood. Ride the caged elevator to the fourth floor. Big, light studio lined with books. Windows facing southwest, with the view of Oakland almost hidden by tall trees. The street noise that used to keep me awake. Home. There was a message from Peggy:

Hey. Are you back yet? Didn't know if you were spending the night. (pause.) I'd like to talk. It's probably time to come clean (laughs).

Checked my e-mail. Also from Peggy: Call me as soon as you get in.

And I did, but she wasn't there. Phone tag.

I decided to call Dean Centro. Searched my desk, found the card that Peggy had given me. It still took a good ten minutes to get a real voice. Ms. Real Voice then put me through to Mr. Centro. I noticed an Italian accent, but barely. No, he wasn't officially handling Peggy's affairs. He'd been a friend of Thomas's. He was just helping out. At this point instinct told me to go into my dumb poet routine.

"Actually, I'm calling because Peggy says she trusts you. I have this CD, and it isn't making much, and I don't know what to do with it. I'm a poet, and you know how we can be with money."

"We have people who can handle that for you. They make it pretty simple."

"That stuff is never simple to a poet."

"OK. Any friend of Peggy's . . . but I'm off soon. Why don't you meet me at Café Roma, around 5:30? You can tell me what you've got, and what you expect to make. I'll bring some information for you."

Roma is very crowded at that hour, and there's no full bar. I got an espresso and found a table in the back room. People use that area as office space. Laptops and cell phones. At least it's quiet. I was a bit early. I had a strategy meeting with that con-man part of my brain. I would continue to play dumb. Only mention trinkets if absolutely necessary. At this point in the game nobody knew I was involved. I could safely assume that Peggy got my name from the pomo lit crowd. Some connection to that job I did for Stephen Rodefer's friend. The poetry world is pretty insular, and there are worlds within that world. The pomo poets have little truck with the beats, and they don't speak to the academics. God help the detective who tries to get straight info out of that little subculture. Hart Denby, for instance, would have no idea that I do these little jobs.

Dean Centro would be wearing a white dress shirt and khakis. I spotted him and waved. I noticed that there were no pleats in the pants. They were, however, quite obviously pressed. He's an amazing specimen. About 5'10," olive skin, hair bleached by the sun (sunlamp?). The kind of body awareness that borders on arrogant. He ordered a single espresso and carried it over in one hand. Like they do in Milano, or so it seemed. We shook, and our hands fit together like a glove. Suddenly I was in a foreign movie. He had green eyes. Sad, questioning, Giancarlo Giannini expression. We sat down and he put his soft briefcase on the desk. Pulled out a few pamphlets.

"All these funds are rather vanilla. You won't make a huge return. But the risk is fairly low. I assume this is for retirement?"

I sensed an angle. I could say yes, and that would be that. I decided to push things a little, see what he was selling. "Mr. Centro, I have about twenty thousand to invest. If I could double that in a few months, I'd do it. I'm ready to take some risks."

He smiled, and the pamphlets were returned to the briefcase. "How well did you know Thomas?"

"I was closer to Peggy. But we got along well."

"Did you know about his collecting?"

"A little. It was mentioned. But I never saw the art pieces. Is that what they were?"

"Not quite. Well, some could be called art. He called

them trinkets. And they were, so to speak, this and that."

"I don't understand."

"There were, for example, the strigils."

"The?"

"Strigils. After working out at the public baths, an ancient Roman would smear olive oil on his body." Centro smiled, leaned closer. I felt myself blushing.

"Go on, Mr. Centro."

"Please. Dean. Or even Dino."

"Go on, Dino."

"As I said, this ancient Roman would cover his body with oil. Then he would scrape the oil, dirt, and sweat from his skin with his trusty strigil, a thin shoehorn-shaped bronze blade. A good collection of strigils can command a handsome price."

It was my turn to lean forward. "Do you think I should invest in strigils?"

"Not exclusively. For example, there are unguentaria."

"Do tell, Dino." Dino's eyes were dilated. He's sexy as hell, and I wanted to think that he was getting off by flirting with me. But I knew it had more to do with Roman beauty products.

"An unguentarium is a little bottle. It's where the Romans kept their perfumed oils. And there are the Etruscan treasures. Little statues that fit in your hand. And jewelry and surgical tools."

"Is it legal to buy and sell these things?"

"Quasi-legal at best." He shrugged. He looked me up and down. "You are a poet, so I thought this would interest you. Poets take risks, right?"

"That's the stereotype. We're also terrible business people. And I'd hate to end up in jail."

"Have you ever been in jail, Clay Blackburn?"

"A few times. Civil disobedience type stuff. I trashed a police car during the Gulf War."

"Perhaps you learned, in your journey through the legal system, that prosecutors give certain crimes low priority. Even if you were caught investing in this, um, scheme, you wouldn't go to jail for long."

"Why not?"

He lifted his hand to his dress shirt and pulled on his white collar. "I'm European, from a good family. Italian-Swiss. I'd get you a good lawyer." Then he brought the hand down, and placed it carefully over mine, his pinky brushing the lip of my espresso cup. He turned my hand over and playfully slapped my wrist. Shrugged again.

I told him that I was interested, but that I needed more information before I gave up my money. He was vague. Some things were coming on the market, and he needed capital to acquire them. He could sell them for a three hundred per cent markup, within a few weeks. If I chose, I could take my payback in trinkets. Or, better for me, he would handle the buy and the resale and pay me $40,000 on my twenty.

I was told that I had a couple of days to think on it. He'd call me. We walked out together. He hugged me goodbye, and as he did he kissed my neck. If I'd had the money with me, I'd have waved it in his face until he promised to follow me home. Sadly, I knew that his flirtations were part of the con.

8.

No messages from Peggy. I called and again. Got the machine. Modern life. Fred's market for a Pacifico, Bongo Burgers for a Persian Burger. A crazy says that, no, Jerry Garcia is not dead.This news flash is worth a quarter and two nickels. Decided to eat dinner on the roof of the Chandler. Postcard view of the Golden Gate, starting to fog over. Gray skyline. Pleasant breeze off the Bay. Nice place to live. Wonder where I'm going with the Peggy thing. The money hunt seems silly. Either the money's spent, or I'm in over my head and will never find it. I suppose there could be some trinkets floating around. What do I know about trinkets? When I finally get to talk to Peggy I'm going to back out. She can talk to a real detective. Shouldn't mix romance and business. And for me romance always comes first.

I finished the Persian Burger as the fog was getting uncomfortably cool. Went back to the apartment. Peggy's key right there on the desk. Then into my pocket. I tried to call one last time. No answer. Maybe she's on the computer. Maybe I'll just go over and check on the cat . . .

By the time I reached the lake it was getting pretty cool. I knocked, then again, then louder. Used the key. Cold inside too. All the windows were open, to my surprise. No meow. The cat must be hiding in the closet again.

Before I did these jobs I had little everyday involvement with death. At estate sales, I would have to speak with the bereaved. Affect a serious countenance, shake hands, make my offer. I'd lost my share of friends and relatives, but they were off camera, so to speak. They say that homicide detectives are completely hardened to death. Smoke a cigarette, drink a Coke, check out the scene, break for lunch. I'm not quite that hard. Not yet. And this was Peggy.

She was lying on her stomach, head twisted to one side. An unnatural pose. I touched her, and she was cold. A different type of cold. Only the dead feel like the dead. I had a childhood memory of kissing a very old relative goodbye, as she slept in an open coffin. Like kissing dry ice, or metal so cold that your lips could stick. The dead have touched me in a few places now. Once I had occasion to cut a man down from a tree. He'd been hanging for at least a day. As he fell, his shoulder touched my forearm. Another time, I pulled a bloated body from the ocean, near San Pedro. Much later we found that it was a woman. Since then my hands always seemed too cold. I bent down and kissed Peggy. Dead Peggy. Peggy's corpse. Then I went over to the couch, put my face in my hands, and caved in.

For awhile. Sort of half asleep. I shook myself, and paced around the apartment, but away from the windows. There was lots of traffic on the street. Had anybody noticed me? Doubtful. Thousands of cars, people hurrying home from work, talking on their cell phones, thinking about other things. I hadn't noticed any pedestrians. Or neighbors. I checked out the apartment. There had been a struggle. Blood in strange places. The closets had been emptied onto the floor. Drawers were open. The cops would call it a robbery, do a routine investigation. I could call and play the good citizen. What good would it do? It would be a great risk for me. I'm getting pretty good at my new job. The secret to my success comes from being a fly on the wall. Nobody would dream that I'm a . . . whatever the hell I am. American poets have two things in common: we are anonymous, and we are useless. I've learned that there's a kind of power in that. The I, Claudius factor. Lose that, and I lose my new source of income.

I didn't worry about fingerprints. Mine would be everywhere. Yes, officer, we were old friends. I visited once in awhile. These investigations never go too far anyway. I was sure that the real motive had something to do with empty bank accounts and Italian trinkets. But the overworked Oakland police wouldn't dig that deep. Just another robbery/murder on the Lake.

Gertrude the cat came out of the closet and went over to Peggy. Sniffed. I felt a wave of emotion, then I did something stupid. I scooped up the cat and wrapped her in my jacket. She didn't fight much. I walked out of the apartment, where, even in daylight in a heavily populated area, nobody would notice a man leaving a murder scene, carrying a cat in his jacket. I got in the Miata, told Gertrude to ride shotgun, and drove down to Emeryville. I drove past the Watergate Apartments, past the Chinese Restaurant, down to the water. I didn't want to have to explain having a key. And I didn't want Dean, or Stephie, or Hart to know that I was so close to Peggy. Needed to stay anonymous. I left Gertrude in the car and walked out onto the pier, and I dropped Peggy Denby's key into the bay.

I stayed at the Chandler for a week or so. Marvin sold

the math books to Moe's, and I had some cash left over
from Peggy's six hundred. I could afford to hide out. I
turned off the phone. Didn't check the mail. I shuffled
from the roof to the studio to the laundry room. Ate delivery food.

On the eighth day I woke up and went down to the
Miata and took Highway 1 as far as Cambria. It was dan-
gerously foggy around Big Sur, but I drove fast. The Miata
is a dumb car, but it steers well. Death was just beyond the
passenger's side, a few hundred feet, straight down to the
Pacific. I came close to going over on one of the bridges.
Slippery road. I pulled in at Nepenthe and had two over-
priced Negronis to make the drive more challenging.
Came close again, then pulled over at Lucia and put the
top down. By the time I reached San Simeon I was soaked
from the fog spritz. I found a motel near the ocean.
Checked in, called Marvin so that he'd know where to
reach me, walked the beach. Sea otters were clanking
mussels together, opening them up and feasting. A thick
marine layer kept everything cool and gray. I walked until
I got hungry, then had seafood at a seaside bar/restaurant.
Watched TV, walked the beach again, went to sleep. The
next morning I ran the beach until exhausted. Training.
For four days I ran, walked, did sit- ups and push-ups,
watched TV, ate fish. And made plans.

On the fifth morning Marvin called with the information
I needed. Some names and addresses. I checked out of the
hotel. I drove to a little toy store in Watsonville and bought
a couple of Mexican wrestler's masks and a toy gun. Then
I drove to the Capitola mall, where I found a suburban sex
shop. I bought some leather cuffs in various sizes. I put it
all in a daypack and drove to Seabright Beach. A few people know my face in Santa Cruz, but I wasn't likely to see

anybody out at Seabright. It was mid-afternoon and the
June fog had cleared. I parked the Miata a couple of blocks
from the beach. I stopped at a deli and got a turkey sand-
wich and an Orangina to go. I ate on the steps that lead
down to the beach. Lots of tourists, but Seabright never
seems too crowded. I walked down to the water line and
found a nice piece of driftwood. About the size of a club. I
put it in my daypack. I looked south to the yacht harbor
and watched the boats come and go. And I got things
straight in my mind. I took the bus to downtown Santa
Cruz, because a red Miata is a dead giveaway. The transit
center was a minor risk. Clay! What are you doing here?
Just checking on some books, that's all, nice to see you . . .
but I didn't see any familiar faces. After a short wait I
caught the Felton bus. Out through the east side of town
and into a dense rainforest. Beautiful, strange country.
Hiding place for old hippies, drug dealers, mass murderers.
And now, or so I'd heard, second homes for tech yuppies.

His name was Trak. He was a rich kid type who
attended UCSC, off and on. Stevie had told Marvin that
the merchants didn't like him much. A little too rowdy. He
often hung around with Hart, which seemed kind of
strange. Hart's boys are usually artsy and fey. Trak could
play a Nazi in a WWII movie. A strapping blond.

His place was across the San Lorenzo River, by a
small bridge, and near the banks. The house was familiar.
I'd attended parties on this street twenty, twenty-five years
ago. Back then the houses were rickety, populated by a
strange mix of river-rat hippie and punk. Everybody grew
and consumed lots of pot, so the style was very relaxed.
Second-hand sofas on the porch, lots of dogs. The houses
smelled of mildew, mixed with various exotic types of
smoke.

The town had indeed changed. The houses had new windows, new paint, Ikea lawn furniture. The place stank of tech money. I found the address and went around to the back. I wasn't sure where I was going to do on this visit. I might just case the place. I might break in and search for . . . evidence? Trinkets? My hunch was that he and/or one of his friends was involved in the strigel trade. My ultimate goal was to scare him into spilling some information, maybe even pointing me to the killer. I checked out the windows and the doors. If I found him home, I'd do it by force. Otherwise I'd have to gaslight him somehow.

As luck would have it, he was in his backyard, facing the river, sitting on a lawn chair drinking a Beck's. I spotted him as I came around one side of the house, about a hundred yards away. I slowly, quietly unzipped the daypack and pulled out a wrestler's mask. This one was white with silver trim. Then I pulled out the other and put it in my back pocket, along with a handkerchief, the kind that Labrador retrievers wear. I pulled out the driftwood and put the pack back on my shoulder. I walked, slowly and quietly, up to him. He didn't turn. I hit him, very hard, just at the base of the skull. He turned toward me with a funny smile. I hit him again. I'd aimed for the temple, but I shot low and got him in the ear. I felt myself cringe. That must have really hurt. He slumped over, and I came around and kicked over the flimsy chair. He fell hard. He looked half out, eyes not quite focused. Once upon a time I boxed. Not pro. Golden Gloves. When you see that look in your opponent's eyes you know you've won. Unfortunately, I also know how it feels to be that far gone. I wasn't the greatest boxer. I slipped the second wrestler's mask over his head, backward. I cuffed his hands behind his back. Cuffed his left leg to the picnic table. I hit his right kneecap a good shot with the driftwood. He wouldn't kick me with a broken leg. I sat down in his newly vacated chair and finished his beer, and waited for him to come to. After awhile he started to stir. I'd decided to do my Truman Capote Key West queer imitation.

"Thank you for the beer, sir. A few questions and I'll leave you be."

"Fuck you."

I felt a little sick inside. He was going to be feisty. I began to hate myself for doing this. I pushed those feelings down. He had to be really frightend, scared out of his wits. That was my only chance of getting information. I stuck the barrel of the toy gun into the bleeding wound on the back of his head. Pushed hard. "I'm going to kill you if you don't answer a few simple questions. I know how, and I don't like you."

I heard the beginning of a whimper, or something. A terrible sound. He'd cracked.

"OK. Anything you want."

"Who killed Peggy Denby, and why?"

"She got herself killed."

"How so, sir?" I was laying the Capote act on thick.

"She came at us. We were supposed to get the strigils, that's all. We didn't think she'd be home. She came at us! Screaming. She threw things. She womped Weldon with a tiki torch. He was bleeding like a stuck pig. It became a free-for-all. I didn't know she was dead until Hart called yesterday."

"Who's Weldon?"

"My partner. But he's gone. Left town. You can kill me, I won't tell you where."

I decided to let that one go. "Did Hart hire you?"

"Yes."

I heard voices upriver. Hikers. I needed to learn more, but I had to beat it fast. I tied the handkerchief around his head, covering his mouth. Only a semi-effective gag, but it would have to do. I packed my things and left, back to the bus stop, back downtown, back to Seabright. I deposited the daypack and its contents in the beach dumpster, after smudging any possible prints. Not that it mattered. Mr. Trak wouldn't be going to the police.

A little more than an hour later I was hunting for parking in Berkeley traffic. I found a semi-legal place on Regent Street, close to home. When I entered the Chandler Gertrude ran up to me like a dog. I fed her, then I made myself a Negroni. My hands were shaking. I'd risked killing somebody to satisfy a hunch. What if I'd been wrong? Too late to think about that. I wasn't wrong. Unfortunately, circumstances hadn't allowed me to get all the information I needed. Halfway through the drink I allowed myself to feel a sense of satisfaction. I'm not a very nice person, I guess. I enjoyed bruising that strapping young man. Even a broken leg doesn't mean much to someone so young. And he didn't even get a glimpse of me.

I checked my messages and my e-mail. There was a memorial reading for Peggy planned for Sunday at the Small Press Distribution Warehouse. That's not as strange as it seems. SPD is a nonprofit. They distribute (or try to distribute) our chapbooks and our magazines. Nobody else would. In effect, the SPD warehouse is where our poetry goes to die. A perfect place for a poet's funeral.

I went to Andronico's for steak and red wine. I owed Marvin many good dinners. I didn't have the energy to do something elaborate, but I knew he'd appreciate a New York, very rare. He'd come into the kitchen, see the steak warming to room temperature on the counter, say, "That's not very Berkeley of us," and smile.

And so he did. And then he took his place in the dining room, the one with the best view of the hills. I brought out the steak, salad, bread.

"Do you think you broke his leg?"

"Not really, although the adrenalin was flowing. I probably hit him pretty hard."

"The wrestling mask is usually reserved for surer cases. You didn't really have much to go on. I'm surprised you didn't just talk to him."

"I'm pissed off. And I don't like the idea of frat boys in Felton."

"Still . . ."

"Let's change the subject. Who is Weldon?"

"According to Stevie he runs with Hart and company. Helps him schlep books, does work around the house. I don't think you should waste too much energy on him. Let him go, unless you want revenge. If your mind is on strigils, or getting to Hart, Weldon would just be a waste of time."

"Where do I go from here?"

"Depends on what you want."

"I want to fuck with Hart."

"Kill him?"

"You know that's not my style. I'd like to get the strigils. Maybe find the evidence to put him away. That is, if I can do it and stay anonymous. I don't want him or the cops to know that I'm involved. After this adventure I'm going back to full time book scouting."

"I've heard that before."

9.

The SPD warehouse is down on Seventh Street, in an area that was once an industrial wasteland. You know how it works: Artists move into a depressing industrial area to take advantage of the cheap loft space. The artists need a café. The café draws student "bohemian" types. A nice restaurant opens. Soon there is a full-scale yuppie attack, and the artists are priced out. At this writing the neighborhood is about halfway ruined. There's still a nice junkyard, and there's enough violent crime to keep the place honest. But not for long.

As I approached the warehouse I noticed little clumps of poets, grouped by school. There's a group without a name, mostly from the Mission District in San Francisco. They were smoking cigarettes out by the gutter. A couple of old Surrealists were holding court near the front door, dressed in salvation army suits. The language poets, our turn of the century avant-garde, stood silently off to the side. They were well dressed, in a scholarly way.

I entered the building. There's a little reception room up front, lined with small press books. I looked for one of mine, found a copy of *Selected Poems 1984-90* (Hardball Press) and smiled to myself. The room was crowded with people, and a little too warm. I hugged Gloria Frym and waved Hi to Ishmael Reed. Then I pushed my way to the warehouse area. It's a bright, clean space. Shelves had been moved and chairs had been set up. A good-sized crowd was milling about. Tragedy brings out the poets. Especially an early death. We eat it up. Until the age of thirty we pray that we'll die young. Most of us push the issue, in various ways. After thirty we feel regret. An untimely death is the poet's best chance at fame. Immortality is the driving force for us.

It was surprisingly stuffy, given the high ceilings. I saw Marvin come in, talking to Stephen Ronan. Then right behind them Hart, with his sister, Stephanie. I'd remembered seeing her somewhere, but I couldn't place where. She looked unhappy and out of place. I sympathized. Not that I really felt out of place. But I would have liked to. These poetry gatherings are like family reunions. I look around and say, I am not like these people. Then I say it again, and again. And then, I cut the crap. When I stop resisting, I realize that, like it or not, I'm at home with these folks. I share the jealousies and the marginalization and the self-hatred that surfaces when you realize that you are not a useful member of society. But I also share their sense of defiance. Poets are a pissed off bunch. I like that.

It took a long time to get us to come to order. I found a seat next to Michael McClure, behind Hart and Stephie. Jack Foley MC'd. One by one, Peggy Denby's friends read their poems. They were earnest and sincere in their delivery. But the poems seemed hollow. Double-bubble lingo-babble. Poetry has become either overly sentimental (Maya Angelou) or maddeningly abstract (Ashbery). There should be a contemporary poem for every wedding and funeral. This is our work. But we've chosen to give humanity short shrift. I closed my eyes and thought of

Peggy, and the words became a blur. In softer focus, the poems seemed more helpful. The human voice can be soothing, regardless of content. The voices washed over me and I thought of sitting on her floor and talking all night. I thought of all the possibilities. She was the one, I thought. Or at least one of the ones. We would have stayed in each other's lives for a long time. For a time I tried to imagine that all the voices were hers. I came became conscious of the readers again as Michael Price came to the podium. Rather than read a poem of his own he quoted Ed Dorn, and I was reminded of the greatness of verse:

> And so you are mortal
> after all said I
> No mortal, you describe
> yourself
> I die, he said
> which is not
> the same as Mortality

And the lights went up, and there was a low murmur. Stephanie turned to me with a "Do I know you?" smirk. She had sensibly short brown hair. She was tall. She was wearing expensive clothes, the kind that come from online catalogues. There was a beautiful leather jacket slung over her seat. Here eyes were brown and almond shaped. She had a perfumey scent, rare in Berkeley, where perfume is considered an affront to those with allergies. Hart introduced us and she shook hands in a business-like way. She was definitely not my type. We'd have different values, nothing to talk about. I wanted to fuck her. In fact, I would have cut off any given finger with a chef's knife for the chance to fuck her. This was not the appropriate time to be feeling these things. Which made the feeling stronger. I was sweating, and my eyes were probably dilated. People were shaking hands and saying "Hi." People who I hadn't seen in years, people that I care about. They annoyed and distracted me.

I followed them outside and tried to make small talk. They said that they were in a hurry. Hart turned to say hello to Lyn Hejinian, and as he did Stephie slipped me her business card.

It was late Sunday afternoon. I circled my apartment for nearly an hour, with post-memorial tears in my eyes. Finally I took a place near Shattuck Avenue, many blocks from the Chandler. On the walk to my apartment I bought a *Street Spirit*, the newspaper of the Bay Area homeless, from a woman with two teeth. When I was out of her sight range I threw it in a dumpster. Sometimes I read the *Spirit*. Often I can't. If I read every issue I'd eventually become a terrorist, which would be a good thing for the world-at-large. Not so good for me.

I stopped at my apartment to feed the cat, then went straight to the roof. It was clear in the East Bay. San Francisco was fogging in again, in that postcard way. I decided to try to remember as much as I could about Peggy. Every reading, every party. Every late night that we spent drinking McCallen's or Glenfiddich, discussing everything. I drifted for a long time. After awhile I thought about the strigil situation. Decided to give it all up, then decided to stay with it. Too curious. And I knew that Hart had a hand in it. I didn't think Trak was lying about that. There had to be some justice. Or revenge. Or something.

I still had Stephie's card in my top pocket. I told myself that she might have some information. That I should call her. After a few seconds I stopped lying to myself about the reason.

"Well, well. Clay Blackburn. Are you asking me on a date?"

"I suppose so. You did give me your card."

"So I did. Can you come this afternoon? We could have coffee somewhere over here."

She gave me an address in Montclair. I have a good sense of direction, and I know the East Bay. Still I got lost. The house was up a few hills and behind a few trees. You couldn't quite call the driveway a private road, or maybe you could. There was an L.A. style lawn and a porch the size of my apartment. I remembered hearing somewhere, probably from Hart, that there had been a rich husband. Hearn somebody. No. Somebody Hearn. Stephanie Hearn. I think she used his name. I couldn't remember his name because I kept getting stuck on Lafcadio. Probably no relation.

She was wearing a white fuzzy sweater. The kind that you don't see in Berkeley. Short dark green skirt. Khaki, but upscale khaki. No pleats. If I sold the Miata I could probably buy her a pair of shoes. Expensive shoes stand out in an obvious way. I once bought a pair in Rome. I wear them when I need to look like a rich person. Doesn't matter what I wear with them. Stephie's shoes were dark and plain, but the heels were built to make all the muscles in her legs behave in a sexual way. They were well-exercised legs, but they hadn't seen a lot of sun. Milky Irish skin. A strange match with the almond eyes.

She met my gaze. I remembered that Hart has those eyes. Yet, in Hart's face they look too small and beady. What a difference a head makes. She ushered me in and we were silent for awhile. It seemed like a long time. To break the ice I asked her about her work. I'd remembered something about her and computers. She went into a long monologue about e-tailing. First she started a company that sold exercise videos on the web.They'd take a profile, then they'd pair the customer with the best video. They raised enough capital to make a good start and then they were bought by a bigger company. She took her earnings (her word) and founded (her word) a company that sold chocolate made by a small Belgian factory. They were bought out by Whitman's, and will soon be part of the K-Mart website. Then she bought into . . .

"Before we go on with the résumé, perhaps we could go out for a drink?"

"I'll make you something here. But I won't join you yet. I have a hard and fast rule: never drink before sun-down. If you do, run straight to AA."

"Whatever you do, don't summer in Stockholm." She didn't acknowledge the joke. I think, on some level, she did understand that she was in the presence of another human being. But I'm not entirely sure. Not everyone has a soul.

We went into the kitchen. Hanging copper pots, huge cutting table in the middle of the room. Restaurant-quality stove. But no bar area. Elegant houses used to have bars. The world is going to hell in a handbasket.

"What would you like?"

"Do you have Campari?"

She opened a cupboard. A bottle of Campari peeked out from behind a bottle of Sapphire Gin. Fitting.

"I'll have a Negroni."

"What's that?"

"I figured you'd know, since you have Campari."

"Once a year I go to Bevmo and buy a few cases of everything. For the Christmas party. I'm not even sure what I have. For myself, I just pour some vodka in a big glass and top it off with tonic."

"Aren't you from that new cocktail generation?"

"I don't think so. I'm too old. When I was in college we drank rum and fruit juice. I go to the new bars after work sometimes. But I don't pay much attention."

She was boring, plodding, without subtlety. They all are. Too much screen time. Computers have turned us all into lab rats, pressing the right button to elicit the proper response. That's what passes for interactive. Was my attraction to her sadistic or masochistic? Probably it was beyond psychology. It had more to do with scent, although her scent was rather bland. Maybe it was a class thing. Like *Swept Away*. But that sort of thing didn't usually appeal to me. Oh well, she had given me an opening.

"I could teach you how to make a perfect Negroni. Would you like that?"

"Is that something I should know?" When she asked she almost sounded sincere.

"A good Negroni is life's second best sensual pleasure." And thank god, she didn't ask 'What's first?'

"All right. You teach me. I'll have one too. It's nearly sundown. I guess I can cheat by a few minutes."

I started by slicing the lime that I found in her oversized reefer. I found a great martini set and put it on the cutting table. Bought, she said, on Ebay. Forties vintage. Simple pitcher, long glass stirrer, oversized glasses. Clear. First rule: no tinted glass. Ruins the color. I found the vermouth and put half a shot in each glass. She came behind me and looked over my shoulder. She was just a little shorter than me. Her chin touched the back of my neck. I swirled the vermouth, then poured it in the sink. Made her smell a glass. That's all you need of the vermouth. I poured a shot of Campari into the bottom of the pitcher. I filled the pitcher with ice. I poured three shots of the good gin over the ice, slowly. Swirled the ingredients until cold. Poured them into the glasses. Added a small squeeze of lime and dropped a wedge in each glass.

She was delighted by the color. She took a sip and made a face.

"Strong."

"That's the point. It's sort of like drinking a single espresso. A strong shot of flavor, and a condensed version of the drug."

She shrugged and gulped. We moved to a living room area, to a big couch. The kind of couch that you see advertised in SF *Weekly*. SOMA Sofas. I sat down and I wanted to move in. The white leather was cool and then warm. She put on some music. A sound that I took to be the Dave Matthews Band. Although it could have been somebody else. That kind of music bores me. We finished our drinks and she volunteered to make another.

"What if I make them stronger?"

"They won't taste right. But we'll get drunker."

She dumped an extra shot in the pitcher. We took the drinks back to the huge white couch. We drank, and she spoke of many things. None were of much interest. IPOs, stock options, new economic opportunities. The language of this particular California gold rush. She told me that the house was part of the divorce settlement. He owned three, and an apartment in Vienna. It was an amicable split. He still stops by when he's in town. He's mostly in Eastern Europe, finding new markets. For what, I don't know. Didn't seem worth asking. I didn't mention the strigil situation, or Peggy. Couldn't find an opening.

There was another round, and then we were horizontal on the couch. She was on top, and I felt like I was swimming in leather and skin. She was, to my surprise, very good. Better than I am, if you want to look at things that way. I was surprised that it had been so easy. And that I was so attracted to someone that I really didn't like. It took awhile to hear that certain click that I hear when the rational part of the brain goes dead and nature takes over. But eventually I did hear the click, and we stayed on the couch for a long time.

She asked me if I wanted another drink. I took this as an invitation to spend the night and said yes. We took the last drink into the bedroom. Beige and black Ikea. Not as obviously expensive as the living areas. A framed Thiebaud print over an oversized bed. A little like a hotel room in Sonoma. I wasn't really listening to what she was saying but her voice was sounding more pleasant. I still didn't like her, but I was taking her more personally.

10.

I spent less and less time at the Chandler. I'd put in some quality time with the cat, make some calls, and go out searching for books. Marvin suggested that I disguise Gertrude by fattening her up. She was kind of sleek when I took her from Peggy's apartment three weeks ago. I put her on a diet of Yoplait, Ben and Jerry's, and cheese omelets. She gained a couple of pounds. He also suggested a funny collar, to throw people off track. I decided on zebra stripes, with a green name tag: Emily. Emily the indoor cat. My friends loved her. Stephie tolerated her. If by chance

Hart were to come over Emily would go in the walk-in.

Marvin also suggested that I stop seeing Yuppie Girl, as he dubbed her. I didn't, although my only real reason was lust. But then, is there a better reason for anything? I'd pretty much ruled her out as a suspect. I would occasionally try to nudge the conversation into strigil territory, but she didn't seem to know much. She was aware that brother Hart was some kind of collector, but it was all very vague.

In the weeks that followed we fell into a pattern. I would go over there. She seldom came by the Chandler. I would cook a nice dinner in her perfect pots, on her perfect stove. We'd go out on the second-floor terrace and look at the Bay, and I'd hear about her stocks, and nod, and wait. Sometimes she'd tell me about something that happened at the office. Usually it had to do with a field trip of some kind. Intrigue at the brewpub, or the billiards place, having to do with what people used to call office politics. The actual work didn't seem to matter. This seemed strange and sad. She confided to me that she had once been very depressed, but that antidepressants had helped a lot. I felt a speech welling up in my throat. Of course you're depressed, your life is depressingly drab. Those feelings are the only sane reaction to the world that you have made. But I let that speech stick in my craw. None of my business, I told myself.

After getting some air we would go to the big white couch. She called her couch Pablo, her bed Eileen. She said they were named after people she'd always wanted to sleep with. We would get comfortable on Pablo and I would sink into a physical rhythm that I have rarely known. It had nothing to do with two souls touching. That romantic conceit has, sadly, been ripped from my heart.

Still, there were times when I thought I was falling for her. Time proved otherwise. It was purely physical. But that's not something to complain about. I'm not really a spiritual being. I'll leave that to the Dalai Lama. For me, consciousness is at its highest at the point of orgasm. Other times come close: staring at a Franz Kline painting, listening to Chopin's 'Nocturnes,' reading *Song of Myself*. But they don't add up to those times when I was on Pablo with a rather blandly beautiful woman named Stephie and then a moment later I wasn't with anyone. I was just a piece of meat attached to another piece of meat, and I closed my eyes and saw colors that you don't expect to see in nature, and we floated like there was no gravity, beyond identity or personality.

Eventually we would start to drift off and she'd say, Time to visit Eileen. And we'd get into her very large bed, between sheets with astronomical thread counts, and under a comforter that cost more than I make in a month. I'd get myself into a position to smell her hair, and I'd fall asleep with my right hand between her legs, at the thighs. She said that boy's hands always seem to rest there when they sleep.

Marvin was getting jealous. I was spending most nights over there. He wasn't getting as many dinners. He doesn't understand these romantic/sexual obsessions. He has people who he sees. That's how he puts it. Men and women, mostly people he's known for awhile. Some are single, others are married. They drift in and out. There always seems to be someone there when he needs company. He doesn't seem to worry about it much. His romantic notions involve the failure of communism. I've seen him in tears over Lenin's death. I try not to mention the Spanish Civil

War. I agree with him, that the failure of international socialism was the great tragedy of the twentieth century. But it doesn't touch me in the same way.

I had to make Marvin a great dinner, or he'd guilt me all summer. I dug out the pasta machine and made noodles tossed with yellow tomatoes from a friend's garden. It's a nice first course. Then I took the Weber up to the roof and smoked a pork loin. Braved the lines at Berkeley Bowl for some nice greens. Bought a large chunk of very good chocolate and a bottle of grappa. His favorite dessert.

He came in and I opened one of two bottles of Tavel that Alice Notley had brought me from Paris. He beamed from ear to ear. We ate a long, slow dinner and drank more than usual. He told me one of those promise-not-to-tell-anybody stories, about how a few days earlier he'd been cut off by an SUV, and he had followed it at a safe distance. It parked at the Andronico's in North Berkeley. And there, in broad daylight, he dragged his key down the side of the car. Then, satisfied that nobody was watching, he keyed the other side. He took a short walk and came back. The SUV was still there. There were people in the lot, but nobody seemed to be paying attention. So he took out his Swiss army knife and punctured a tire.

"I could have lit the car and myself on fire. Nobody'd notice. We live in a strange world. People can't see outside themselves."

"The guy who owns the SUV probably noticed something."

"Yeah, but it was no big deal. He probably called AAA on the cell phone and went on his way."

And so we traded hell-in-a-handbasket stories for awhile. Finally he got on to the subject of Stephie. How I disappoint him, going out with a capitalist slug. I pointed out that she isn't a slug, that she works very hard.

"Hard work? Going to theme restaurants with investors? And I hear from some of my friends in that world that she isn't very good at it. She's in more debt than Amazon. Everything's in hock. People keep pouring money into her companies, because that's what people do. But she needs a winning streak soon, or it'll all dry up. I think you should question her more closely about the strigil caper. Anyone who is that financially vulnerable is suspect."

Marvin had made his point. He was a little smug about it, but I didn't even try to shoot him down. I'd been thinking with my dick. Usually that isn't so bad. I mean, why not? The brain is overrated. It second guesses, it frets, it hides little childhood traumas, it gives itself headaches. The penis points to love, warmth, affection. Most of the time, and for most people, that's just fine. But in this new line of work I have to find a balance between the two. Thinking with my dick could get me killed.

11.

It was my waiter's day off so I ordered a Glenfiddich, straight. Can't ruin it. You just pick up the bottle and pour it in a glass. The student waiter took my order, disappeared for twenty minutes, then brought me the drink. I was sitting outside on the patio, facing away from Telegraph Avenue. From that angle I could pretend to be in the south of France. Trees and an old brick house.

It was time to have a strategy session with myself. Okay. I had fallen for a woman, a poet, kind of nerdy. Marvin would call her a double-bubble lingo-babble poet. But she was cute. And I liked her. We could talk. Smart and funny. She told me half of a story about some money that was missing from her late husband's estate. Mentioned his love of "trinkets." Then somebody killed her in her apartment by an intruder. A hunch told me that it wasn't a random crime, so I used a little force and found that Hart Denby, son of the late husband, was party to the murder. Trinkets figure into this somewhere. I'd been asked to get involved in some scheme to acquire more.

Berkeley is a small city surrounded by big cities. South Berkeley is a village. So it wasn't much of a coincidence when Dino Centro came out to the patio.

"May I join you?"

"Sit down, Dino."

"You were lost in thought."

"I was thinking about Peggy Denby. I miss her."

"I understand you were close."

"We were good friends."

"More than that?"

"No." I was ready to blow my cover and grab him by the collar, make him tell me what he knew. But, as I've said, anonymity is my best defense. I sank back into myself. Remember Clay, one side of my head said to the other, Negative Capability. I decided to nibble at him.

"I haven't had time to think about that investment."

"I assumed you were out of town, since I didn't hear from you."

"Did Peggy have anything invested?"

He started to say something, then he didn't. He sat for a while.

"No. Well, through her husband. She didn't talk about it much. Our friendship was more personal. We gossiped, talked about local politics, things like that. I like contemporary art too, and she was a great date at openings. Why do you ask?"

"This strigil business is, as you said, quasi-legal. Could there be a connection to her murder?"

He looked suitably nervous. Didn't mean anything. Murder makes everybody nervous.

"The people I deal with aren't like that. We're business people. We aren't criminals. I mean, we do break laws. Everyone breaks the law. But these laws are more subtle, and so are we. I've never been a party to any violence."

"But there must be lots of people involved. If someone found out that Peggy had a good cache of trinkets in her apartment, wouldn't that be a motive for, at the very least, a burglary? Breaking and entering is risky business. Maybe things got screwed up, and violence turned out to be Plan B."

"You haven't talked to the police?"

"I never talk to the police. And you know the cops aren't going to look too deeply into this one. Unless they know about the trinkets."

He was one hard question away from losing his cool. I let him stew for a couple of minutes, then a couple of minutes more. I looked for the waiter. Ordered two scotches.

"Peggy was our friend. I'd like to know who is responsible. Wouldn't you?"

"Of course, of course. But I don't know. I have no idea who killed her. There may have been some items in the apartment. I'm not sure."

The drinks came quickly, to my surprise. He took a healthy gulp.

"If I tell you what I know you will go to the police."

"As I said, I never talk to cops. I'd just like to satisfy my own curiosity."

"Are you a detective or something?"

"Of course I'm not a fucking detective."

"The last cache of artifacts is missing. If you come across it I'll split it with you."

"Missing since when?"

"Thomas inspected them in Italy. Soon after that they vanished. A mix of things, from a dealer in Livorno. Included were an exquisite Etruscan figurine, a few strigils, some Roman kitchen utensils, some surgical tools. Our richest load."

"Worth?"

"About ten years salary at the bank. I'm from a good family, but they've cut me off. A few indiscretions." He closed his eyes. A look of beatitude came over his face. "Imagine," he said, "a spatula that was used to sauté onions and peppers at the forum!"

"Dino, you devil."

He sucked at his drink. "If we get to be friends, I could tell you stories." He leaned forward. Some people are sexier when ruffled. Not Dino. He looked puffy and sad.

"I doubt that I'll ever come across your strigils. I'm going to back away from that. I only asked you about Peggy because, as I said, I'm curious."

"I think you're more involved than you let on, Clay."

"Why?"

"I was on Solano Avenue the other night. I saw you coming out of Ajanta with Stephie. Holding hands." He flashed a comic lurid smile.

"What's Stephie got to do with this?"

"She's heavily involved in the trinket trade. Big ticket

items, too. All over the globe." Dino was obviously loving this.

"I had no idea, Dino."

"I almost believe you."

"Really, Dino. The trinket trade is beyond me. And I never discuss money with Stephie."

He laughed. "But money is all she'll discuss! It's all she knows. She isn't like me. Money is my business, but it's just a job. I'm interested in what it will buy. I'm a sensualist, and that gets expensive. Money is a necessary bore."

"Filthy lucre?" I was having fun, too.

"Clean, dirty, neutral. No matter to me. They don't ask when you pay the bill at Chez Panisse. And now it's time for me to get back to the bank and shuffle dollars. Maybe some will stick to me before the end of the day. Remember, if you happen on some trinkets, you bring them to me. I know where to go with them. And I'm discreet."

He leaned foreword again and looked me in the eye. His eyes looked kind of buggy. I think he was trying to flirt. But I was charmed by his silliness. I felt myself blush.

"I've heard about you, Clay."

For a second I thought that he was referring to some of my bisexual adventures. Then it dawned on me. He'd heard about my little jobs. Blown cover.

"And who else knows?"

"Don't worry, Clay. I heard from Nanos Valaoritis at the Greek Festival."

"Aren't you Italian?"

"But I love Moussaka! Nanos says that you once found some Cavafy manuscripts that were stolen from a rare book dealer. I think most of the poets in town know your game.

"Luckily nobody listens to poets."

"Lucky for you, yes. Because Hart probably hasn't gotten wind of it. You make him nervous as it is."

"Hart hangs out with poets."

"But they don't like him much. To a poet, every non poet is a philistine. Publishers, translators, editors, the UPS guy . . . all philistines."

"What about you? How does a banker gain entrée into this nether world?"

"I once lived with Harold Norse. He is a great gossip. And, I am told, a great poet. I don't read poetry myself. Harold introduced me to everyone. You're a fascinating lot."

I vaguely remembered that Harold had lived with a young Milanese businessman. I think, maybe. Keeping track of Harold's lovers would be a full-time job.

Dean Centro stood up, rather abruptly. "Time to get back to the bank." We shook, and his hand lingered in mine. He'd calmed down a bit, and the buggy-eyed look softened to a classic Latin-lover narrowing of the eyes and a whispered, "You have my number."

I ordered a single espresso, just to linger. Stephie was involved, Peggy was possibly involved. Hart and Trak are murderers, as is somebody named Weldon. Dean Centro is a crook. And I am a dubious character. I turned my chair around to look at the Avenue. Pale sunlight. The kind that comes right after the fog fades back. Across the street, three exquisite college students were heading toward Bison Brewery. I couldn't make out their tattoos, but they had them, and long dreads. And as the dark-haired woman kissed the blond man, her girlfriend, who I took to be East Indian, leaned on her, back to back, and I tried to freeze the moment. I didn't want to move into the future just yet. But the moment wouldn't freeze.

13.

Saturday morning I hit the garage sales. I hate them, but my stock was getting low. I needed fodder. Fodder is pocketbooks, popular novels, dictionaries. Normal stuff that I can use for quick cash at the trashier used book stores. I put together three bags of stuff, possibly a day's pay. On the way to Half Price Books I spotted a yard sale on Regent Street. And there, under some Ian Fleming pulp, in perfect condition, was a copy of Campion's Works, edited by Percival Vivian, Oxford University Press, 1909 edition. Not a large book, but hefty. Type so beautiful that I had to blink back tears. I've only seen a few of these. I already own one, so there was no temptation to keep it. I walked over to Ho Chi Minh Park and sat in the cool morning sun, and spent some time with Thomas before taking him to Moe's Books: Fain'd love charmed so my delight/That still I doted on her sight.

I made enough to last a couple of days without raiding the savings account. I stopped in at the Chandler, changed, and walked up Dwight to the track to do a little running. Then I came home and hit the heavy bag. One corner of the studio is my mini boxing gym. Heavy bag, light weights, jumping rope. Very heavy padding on the floor, to keep the downstairs neighbor from complaining.

When I was twelve I boxed Golden Gloves. That first year I lost most of my fights. No punch. Couldn't take a punch either. I'd score well, because I had fast hands. But about midway through the fight the other guy would hit me hard, and I'd go down. I had some courage (stupidity?) so I'd usually get up for my second (or third) knockdown. Then one day Archie Moore came into the gym in Long Beach. He had come up from San Diego to raise funds for his youth group. He saw me take some good shots during a sparring match. It made him laugh. Maybe his plane was delayed, or maybe he was bored, but for some reason he took me aside and worked with me. He didn't teach me how to punch. He said that I was hopeless in that area. But he taught me how to slip punches, how to stay out of range, how to block punches with my arms and hands.

I had reached that age when you realize that adults are a corrupt lot and that the rest of your life isn't going to be a great deal of fun. I was full of adolescent bitterness. I had no heroes. But I had to listen to Archie Moore. It wasn't that he was the ex light heavyweight champion. I couldn't give a fuck about that, at the time. It was the cadence and the timbre of his voice. It was his diction, and his strange word choices. He quoted Shakespeare, Keats, Muhammad Ali, FDR. He made up rhymes as he went along, teaching me to duck and move. He said, "You are one proud white boy, but you probably haven't even heard of Jean Paul Sartre, let alone Kierkagaard. You're probably Irish, but you haven't even read Yeats! Not like that, fake to the right, chump!" Archie Moore's poetry was pretty powerful. I listened to his instruction. I still didn't win many fights, but I rarely went home in pain.

I worked up a good sweat, showered, ordered a Persian Burger from Bongo. Took it back to the Chandler. I was

feeling dramatic so I put on some Lizst. Loud.
Gertrude/Emily joined me for a fry. After dinner I opened
a second Pacifico and went over to the computer to work
on a poem. My daily dose of sanity. I had been at work for
a couple of hours when the phone rang. It was Stephie. I
spent the latter part of the evening on Pablo and Eileen.

I was starting my second espresso when Hart came in.
Stephie had warned me that he might come by for breakfast. He gave me a warm hello but we didn't shake hands.
He went into the big, perfect kitchen and got himself a
demitasse. He was wearing a lemon yellow golf course
shirt and black jeans. I understood the shirt to be an iron-
ic gesture, like wearing an aloha shirt at a South of Market
café. He poured a cup of coffee and drank it standing, next
to Stephie. I was amazed at the resemblance and that he
could seem so ugly to me, and she so alluring. My gaze
shifted from the beady, almost comical gray/almond eyes,
to her strange, mysterious, exotic looking pair.

Hart was jovial in a phony way. It's always a little
strange, meeting your sibling's lover. At least he was trying to be nice. We were nicey-nice, back and forth, and
then he started to feel me out.

"In Santa Cruz you were asking me about Peggy's
financial situation. Did you find out anything interesting?"

It struck me for the first time that Hart and Stephie
were Peggy's heirs. But there couldn't have been much of
an estate, what with the missing money.

"Actually I didn't look very hard. None of my business."

"But you brought it up."

"Because Peggy was upset about it. Now that she's
gone I've forgotten about it. Too many other things on my
mind."

"Like?"

"Like mourning for a dead friend. And book scouting. Writing poetry. The usual."

"I assume that Peggy just spent it. But if you hear anything, I'd like to know."

Stephie seemed unnerved. "Hart, let's get off the subject of Peggy."

And we did. But there were more questions about my life, my living, about Marvin. He was fishing. Instinct told me that he didn't know a thing about my other job. I wasn't sure why he was asking so many questions, but I didn't call attention to that. I decided to just flow with the conversation and play dumb.

Finally talk turned to his career, and I suffered through his résumé. A family trait? He'd designed covers for a couple of Creeley books. Very tasteful, in his words. And he was organizing a writer's retreat down in Cabo. Philip Levine would be there, as would Jorie Graham. And they were trying to convince Pinsky to come down. When he said Pinsky's name he looked skyward and sighed.

"Why would you want to subject that poor country to Pinsky? Doesn't Mexico have troubles of its own?"

"Very funny. Pinsky's poetry is high art. You and your Mission District Telegraph Avenue skuzzy poets wouldn't understand that. I've got things to do. Nice seeing you."

But before he left he straightened out the pleats in his khakis.

My work day consisted of going up to the garage and pulling out twenty Loeb Classics that I'd been sitting on for almost a year. They are an instant sell. I drove down to Moe's Books and sold them for six dollars each. I wanted to have some scratch so that I wouldn't have to scout for a couple of days. I'd decided to get myself some of that strigil money, if only to keep Hart Denby from getting it all. High art, my ass.

I called Dean Centro and he said he'd meet me, this time at Oliveto, downstairs. My Loeb money wouldn't last long there, even downstairs. But I went along with it. I arrived early, as is my habit. Punt e Mes at the bar, same star-quality bartenders. Dean arrived in (I swear) seersucker. I looked deep into his eyes and told him that I was almost ready to invest. Couldn't he tell me more? It's a lot of money.

"Well, not here." He looked around the bar. As far as I could tell nobody was paying attention. I laughed.

"You laugh. But we have to be careful. As you said, there is a lot of money at stake. My apartment is close by. Finish your drink and we'll go there."

And I did. The apartment was directly across College Avenue and upstairs, above a used clothing store. It was the kind of sweatbox that would have gone for two hundred a month before the techno gold rush. A matchbox of a studio with a view of the elevated BART tracks. But it was very expensively furnished. This is a new phenomenon in the Bay Area. There was a double bed with a low, modern Italian style headboard. Little black end tables that looked antique. The Chinese vase was from a specific period of history that you would know, if you were an expert in Chinese history. The tapestry was Indonesian. Even the hotplate was the expensive kind. I've seen them in Sur La Table. I was taken with the rug. It was a saffron color, and showed no signs of wear.

"I have some good beer."

"Yes."

And he pulled two from Belgium from the hotel style reefer. We sat for awhile. I let him think. Finally he nodded to himself.

"If you get me twenty thousand before next week, and a little traveling money, I can double, or perhaps triple your investment within, say, another week."

"Where will you be going?"

He hesitated some more. He downed the beer the way you'd drink a Bud on a hot day. Got himself another.

"Why do you need to know?"

"It's my whole bank account. I'd like to know where it's going."

"Mexico."

"I thought strigils were Italian."

"People will be there."

"What kind of people?"

"People from all over, with treasures from everywhere. A kind of convention. There's a fishing village not far from the Cabos. Santa Catarina. Well, it's even outside of there. There's a hotel on the beach. Caters to the sportfishing trade. It's been booked by people who share my interest. People can come in by boat. The authorities assure us that there will be little or no customs check-in. Those that drive or fly in may have more trouble. But most of these people are seasoned smugglers."

"Strigil people?"

"Whatever you want to call us. Seekers of treasure."

"The treasures of the gray market. A kind of antique road show."

"Gray, black, whatever. You won't see this stuff on PBS."

"So you'll go down there and do some buying."

"And selling, and trading. And there will be a yacht there that will take a few of us over to Mazatlan, where there will be some smaller sessions. From there I'll go to Mexico City, and with any luck I'll come home with a fortune. I have some good product. But I need spending money. And I may want to buy and sell something while I'm there. This is a tightly knit group. It's good form to buy a few things. Primes the pump."

"I have a week to think about this?"

"Say, two days. I have other investors, so either way I can make the trip. But I'd be lying if I said I didn't need your money. I'm a little cash strapped. And cash on hand is always important when traveling in corrupt countries. Which is to say, all countries. I've bought my way out of trouble a few times."

"I'm beginning to feel like a loan shark."

"You can triple your money. Who cares?"

"Let me sleep on this."

When I said the word sleep his eyes got wider. He smiled in a flirtatious way. Somehow people know that I will do almost anything for sex. Almost anything. Dino was cute, but not twenty thousand cute. Still, it occurred to me that I could possibly come out of this with a few blow jobs. I leaned in his direction. Our faces moved closer. We stopped for a fraction of a second, that second where you measure the other person's nose, so as not to collide before the first kiss. But at the end of that fraction he moved back, just an inch.

"How sad that I have another appointment!"

The bastard was teasing me. He wanted his money.

I got back in time to make Marvin dinner. Lots of people were milling around on the Avenue. There was a scheduled demonstration. Berkeley's still good for several a year. Usually they're pretty pathetic. Once in awhile there's a corker. We pushed the dinner table closer to the window. I made some burgers and we got ready to watch the fun. We finished dinner and still nothing had happened. Some punks were drinking out on Dwight Way. And, of course, there were lots of cops. They usually outnumber the demonstrators. We decided to take our wine up to the roof, to get a better view. It was a pretty warm night. On the way out the door I grabbed a chocolate bar. We climbed down to a fire escape, split the chocolate, and settled in to watch the show.

And a great show it was. Marvin had heard that the theme was the automobile. The demonstrators were against them. I imagined that there would be a Critical Mass style bike-a-thon. Those can be fun. It started to get dark. The cops looked a little nervous. These things usually end before dusk. In recent years the cheap, inadequate street lamps have been aided by white Christmas lights, just like Paris. The lights gave the trees and the stores a nice glow. There was an ominous silence. Marvin looked at me and nodded happily. I remembered an old-timer telling me the story of how Paul Goodman once tried to give a speech from a Chandler fire escape. He was interrupted by tear-gas. I hoped that the young anarchists that now organize these things would give the cops hell. Our side hadn't won one in a long time.

It was now flat-out dark and still nothing. A few of my neighbors joined us on the roof. We began clapping in unison and yelling 'Rock 'n Roll!' Some of the cops gave us tough looks. Others smiled. They know their parts.

A couple of the punks started hopping up and down, punching the air with their fists. There was a roar, like when someone hits a home run. A mob came down Dwight, and turned onto Telegraph. It was a substantial crowd. The cops retreated, giving the mob some space in front of Shakespeare & Co. They backed off more, to allow traffic to flow up Dwight, but it didn't. The cops looked pissed. This wasn't part of the script. Someone on my roof said that they were supposed to rally at People's Park, then come down Haste Street, which was closed for this purpose. The cops had been outflanked. Clubs were drawn, but not raised. The Berkeley Police are good at this. They herded the crowd into the middle of the street, in front of Café Med. A crusty bunch of regulars drank espresso at the sidewalk tables. Seen it all before.

An old Toyota came around the corner, pushed and pulled by half dozen people, all dressed in black hooded sweatshirts. They were quite solemn. The crowd began a chant that I couldn't understand. They produced cans of lighter fluid and doused the car. Some of the cops laughed, which clued us in. The car was a prop. Otherwise, batons would have been raised.

The car went up in flames. It was wimpy, it was staged, but it was a beautiful sight. It burned slowly, evenly. They must have drained the gas tank. A tow-truck appeared a couple of blocks away. It got warm down on the streets. People peeled off their sweatshirts, their shirts. Public nudity is often a part of these. People started beating on things: trash cans, the sides of buildings. Tribal sounds. I felt bad for a couple of the less stable homeless people. They looked scared. Probably didn't realize that it was just a show.

Marvin threw his arms around me, and we had a good laugh. We've destroyed two cars in our time. Both police cars. And it wasn't sanctioned by local government. We turned one completely over on the night that Dan White got away with murder. Then one of our cohorts lit it up. Full tank of gas. Boom! During the Gulf War we beat the shit out of another one with a policeman's abandoned baton. I went to jail for that. They caught me running away. But they didn't want to bother to prosecute. Cars are easy to replace.

We went back in and took the stairs down to the street. There was a fine racket, and lots of pretty young anarchists were jumping around in various states of excitement. There was a fratboy contingent, as usual. There would be fights later in the evening. I noticed a familiar face. Trak. I wondered what he was doing in Berkeley. Could that be Weldon with him? He looked familiar. Had I seen him in Tampico? I couldn't trust my memory. I moved closer, but it didn't help. Weldon, if it was Weldon, was a small man of about twenty-five. Short, bleached hair, square jaw, solid arms. They milled around for awhile, apparently got bored, and walked off in the direction of campus.

The street took on the look of a big cocktail party. People laughed and talked in small clumps. The police were more relaxed. A guy in a Mohawk brought coffees to go to a couple of the cops. The show was over, except for the cleanup. I walked Marvin to his truck and returned to the Chandler.

14.

My neighbors were hanging out in the lobby and on the stairs. There was lots of imported beer. I absent-mindedly counted the different brands. Singha, Amstel, Sierra Nevada, something with a green frog on the label. Two rich students were drinking malt liquor. Slumming. Eight types of beer and one bottle of white wine. A woman with a crew cut was smoking a turquoise cigarette, which reminded me (fondly) of high school. I'm getting old for this, I thought, but then what else would I do? I reached the fourth floor and stepped over Mariem and Joanne, who told me, mid-kiss, that there was a party at John and Dina's. Their door was open so I went in to say hello. Somebody handed me a too-full lowball glass. Jack Daniels. Another fond memory from high school. Most of the guests were crowded around the windows that face Telegraph Avenue. At street level two punks were having a half-hearted fistfight in front of the remains of a bonfire, setting up a nice visual. I'm the only poet in the building. My neighbors, at least the nonstudents, are painters, photographers, video artists or conceptual/installation types. The guests were mesmerized. All those artsy brains were twisting the experience into who-knows-what, dreaming up projects that would make them famous, or at least keep them occupied. And, this being Berkeley, they were playing a kind of intellectual game of connect the dots. How does this relate to Adorno? Jung? Emma Goldman? Meher Baba? Johnny Lydon?

One of the punks took a punch just as the low flame turned to toxic smoke. One of the guests hooted. The punk got up, dazed and smiling. I recognized him, noting that his nickname is Smiley. Teresa the painter sidled up to me and we clicked our lowball glasses.

"So, Clay. Tell me. What the hell is a strigil?"

"I hear that the ancients used to scrape their bodies with them."

"Hmm. Maybe this guy isn't as boring as he seems."

"Who?"

"He's in the kitchen. Dino something. Says he's a

friend of yours. And when he says it, he raises one eyebrow. Like this."

And she deftly raised one eyebrow, looking sideways over her shoulder, for effect.

"Teresa, I told you, I only sleep with boys in even numbered years. That means no men for seven months."

"So you dated him last year?"

"We haven't known each other that long."

"Should be one hella New Year's eve. Tell me, Clay, do you sleep with women in even numbered years, or do you give them up for boys?"

"I'll sleep with women for as long as they will have me."

She laughed and drifted off. I made my way to the kitchen, but not before Dina refilled my glass from a bottle of Jack Daniels that was bigger than her head, even if you include about five pounds of red hair.

Dino was leaning against a kitchen counter, talking to Tom Clark.

"Dig it, Dino, Dante came before pasta, before bistecca di Fiorintino! And you mean to say you haven't read him?"

"Well, maybe a little, in school."

Dino saw me and gave me a long hug. Flattering.

"Can we go back to your place? I need to talk to you."

I let him in and turned on a lamp. I turned, and the gun was about a foot from my solar plexus. My first reaction was a laugh. Then I shuddered, then I caught myself and tried to act cool. I noticed that he was trembling.

"Dino, what are you doing?"

"I need that money. Now. I know you deal mostly in cash. I need some of it."

"Cut the Peter Lorre routine. I told you I'm interested in investing."

"New facts have come to light."

"Like?"

"There's a certain figurine. It's been missing for years. Today a friend called to tell me that it will resurface in Mexico. I need another fifteen thousand, give or take, to join the consortium that will buy it. They have a buyer. Six . Enough to make me, uh, us rich. But I have to get to Baja with the money, soon. Before the seller shows up. We have to make plans."

"Tell me more about the figure."

"It was first found in Vinci in the nineteenth century. It was in a villa near Livorno for years. Then it was lost, or stolen."

"And, somehow, Thomas got hold of it?"

"Yes. Unfortunately he died before he could sell."

"Murdered?"

"I don't know. My information is secondhand. And, after all, he was ill. Anyway, it was presumed lost."

"Could it have been in Peggy Denby's apartment?"

"How would I know? I knew nothing until yesterday! But I do know that it will turn up in a little village in Baja within the week. And if I get enough cash I can be part-owner. I have a soft spot for Buenos Aires. It's an expensive place to live, but the sale of the figure could buy me a few years there.

His eyes unfocused as he dreamed, presumably, of the cafés of Buenos Aires. I suppressed the temptation to hum a tango. The gun dropped a couple of inches as his mind drifted. I hit the top of his hand as hard as I could. The gun flew to the bed. I jumped on it, and held it on him. But I could tell by its heft that it wasn't loaded.

"You hurt my hand!"

"Sorry, Mr. Lorre. Does the figure have a romantic name? Like in the movies?"

"No, stronzo. This isn't a movie. I could have tripled your money. But you dilly-dallied. I was trying to help you."

"Let's give it a name. How about Leonardo, since it's from Vinci."

"That's silly. Leonardo was from another period. And the figure is a woman. Possibly a fertility goddess."

"Breasts?"

"Yes, but rather small, for an Italian."

He was smiling, getting into the spirit of naming the figure. Another Kook.

"How about Beatrice?"

"Too obvious, Clay. All right, I will play your game. But only if you promise not to throw me out the window."

"Done."

"We will call her Oriana Fallaci, after the journalist."

"Why?"

"Another Italian woman who does a little traveling."

"Well done, Dino."

"Now, there is the matter of the twenty thousand."

"Sorry, Dino. I just don't have it to give."

"But you said . . ."

"A little white lie."

"Luckily I have another, uh, investor. Can I have my gun back?"

"I handed him the empty gun. Our eyes met. Blond Italians are a problem for me. Can't stay away from them. Even when it's inappropriate. Especially when it's inappropriate!

"I can put some ice on that hand, if you have the time."

"Thank you. Do you have a drink?"

I brought out the Villa Masari grappa. It's a southern drink, but I didn't think this Milanese would mind. He was delighted.

He put off his other appointment till morning. And this an odd-numbered year. Rules are made to be broken.

15.

We slept late the next morning. He took his gun and left around noon. I spent the day reading Cavafy on the roof. I rest on Sundays, Mondays, and most Tuesdays. If I leave the Chandler it's to take a walk to the downtown YMCA for a little exercise. At dusk there was the call to prayer from the little storefront mosque on Dwight, sung through a tinny PA system. It was quite warm. Not just warm for Berkeley. Real heat. I closed my eyes and imagined that I was in Egypt. Noise, bad air, the sounds of the Koran. This could be Cairo, or Alexandria. I needed a change of scenery. After this job, a long vacation.

I went into the kitchen and turned the oven up high. Opened every window in the apartment and turned on a fan. Rolled out some pizza dough. Marvin arrived as I was putting the pizza in the oven. He was tired. He'd done tech work all day. I chided him for working on a weekend, calling him a capitalist lackey. He, in turn, was merciless concerning my night with Dino Centro. I had to take it. No defense, really.

"Centro's only concern is money. He'll sell you out. I hope you didn't tell him any secrets."

"We barely said a word."

"His entire value system is based on money, you know. . ."

Here I chimed in, and we said Marvin's favorite line in unison:

"AND MONEY ISN'T A VALUE."

"But I don't really agree, Marv. He's a sensualist. Money's just the means to an end."

"Hairsplitting. There's no morality in there."

"Sort of like your average American."

And it went on like this until we finished the pizza, along with a fair bottle of wine from Abbruzzo.

It was the eve of Bastille Day. Marvin was going down to Santa Cruz to spend it with some friends. I was invited but declined. A date with Stephie. This was met with more eye-rolling and a final chorus of MONEY ISN'T A VALUE. He left, and I was alone quite early. I brushed Emily, who was looking quite fat. She had been acting kind of blasé of late. I wondered if too much ice cream could hurt a cat. Made a note to take her to a vet soon. I had no idea if she'd had her shots.

16.

It was with much male pride that I purchased a big box of condoms at the Chimes Pharmacy. It had been a physical summer. From Chimes I sauntered down the block to Vino for a bottle of Le Commanderie De Queyret Bordeaux Superieur. A Frank O'Hara poem was just outside the reach of my memory, something about Bastille Day, and another that takes place three days after. I hopped into the Miata, top down, and drove up to the classy part of town.

To my surprise Hart was at Stephie's. She must have seen my look of disappointment. She stood behind him and made a gesture that I took to mean, Don't worry, he's leaving soon.

He was drinking Fischer beer. "We're all French today," he said, and he raised his glass. He seemed a little drunk.

"You seem to be celebrating."

"We got Pinsky."

"Huh? Oh, for the poetry fantasy camp."

"You're just jealous. Nobody would ask you to teach anywhere."

I didn't answer. There was something to what he said.

"Or maybe somebody would, Clay. I'd like to do this full time. If that happens, maybe I can have you down for a reading or something. With a little capital, I could found a school. Fuck Naropa and New College. I could put those beatniks out of business. Get Adrianne Rich to come down. And Levine. Sky's the limit."

When he said the word "capital" I happened to be watching Stephie. A nervous look crossed her face. She caught herself, and smiled blankly. I got the idea that Hart was talking too much.

"Hart, I thought you were going over to the city, to Café Bastille."

"Okay, sis, I'm out of here. I'll leave you to your fuck-buddy."

She shooed him out the door. "Sorry, Clay. He's a bad drunk. I hope he takes the BART."

He'd left half a bottle of Fisher. I got a clean glass and poured myself the rest. There were, as promised, two steaks in the oversized reefer. And a shallot, a baguette, salad makings. I fried the shallot in butter and added a little wine. Arranged and tossed the salad, grilled the steaks on her indoor grill. There was also, as requested, a chunk of blue cheese. The ten-minute French bistro dinner.

After dinner she brought out some Armangnac. It was very good. She was learning how to drink like the yuppie that she was. Lucky me. Unfortunately, the drinks were more interesting than the conversation. Until she got to the subject of her brother.

"He's frustrated. He just hasn't found himself. I mean, he has his books, and the poetry. But that isn't a serious life." After saying this she covered her mouth, embarrassed.

"It's okay, dear. I've never wanted a serious life."

She took the cue. "Yes, that's right, you're happy with that life. But Hart wants, um, well, not exactly more, exactly."

"More's the word. This just happens to be enough for me."

"Right, right. Hart wants some security. That doesn't seem to be an issue with you."

It's more complicated than that, I thought. But I let it pass. How could I explain? I don't understand why I do what I do. But it does feel right. The look of embarrassment left her, and she smiled sweetly. I was growing fond of her. It happens when you sleep with somebody more than once. Partly out of a need to justify the continuing sexual union. But there's another reason, too. Intimacy softens us a little. At least for awhile. The old anarchists were right. If we could somehow be capable of free love the world would be a wonderful place. It is generally agreed that human nature won't allow for this. And yet, and yet . . .

She seemed to sense my contemplative mood and she put on an old Brian Eno CD, one I hadn't heard in a long time. She decided that we should smoke some pot. I don't do that much, but this time I went along. And we floated along on Pablo for hours. It was very strong stuff, I was barely in touch. It crossed my mind that maybe she'd slipped me a Mickey. Who cares, I thought. We slept, or at least I did. Then she woke me up and walked me back to the bedroom. Much later I was lying on my back, trying to remember if I'd just made love. And it came to me that I had, and I dropped off again.

I slept till ten. She had coffee ready. I needed it.

"Did you have a nice Bastille Day?"

"Vive la France. I have a bit of a headache. I'm not used to pot."

"Good stuff. I feel foggy too."

We had a long, slow breakfast. I showered and shaved, got ready to go. She walked me out to the car, hanging close in a white terry robe. She smelled great. When we reached the street my heart sank. The Miata had been munched. Sideswiped. Worse than sideswiped. The passenger side door was almost gone.

"Clay, why didn't you park in the drive?"

"Hart's car was in the way. Shit. This is going to be expensive. Shit." I got in the car and examined the door from the inside. A mess.

"Come in the house, and we'll have it towed."

I got inside and fumbled for my insurance card.

She touched my hand, said, "I know somebody who's really good. He's an old friend of Hart's. He'll do it for cost, for me."

"Really?"

"Don't worry. Your AAA card will cover his towing service. I've got his number right here, somewhere. Here."

I took the card and picked up the phone. I had to restrain myself from laughing and saying, "Something's hinkey here Stephie, what's going on?"

She saw me hesitate. She reached around me from behind and said, "It's okay, Clay. I'll get it fixed for you cheap. Weldon's a great body guy."

17.

Weldon was in fact Weldon, the Weldon that Trak had mentioned under duress. Weldon the murderer, according to Trak. He was waiting in the office of the San Pablo Garage, a nondescript place on a block with futon shops, ethnic markets, and a Taco Bell. It was a long tow from Montclair. I hoped my insurance would cover it. I hadn't questioned Stephie about using her friend's body shop. I wondered if she found that strange. Probably not. People tend to be dazed when these things happen. Open to suggestion. I wondered if some kind of fix was on. Couldn't imagine what the angle might be.

Weldon's look was working class. Lots of tattoos and a haircut that looked like it had been done by a Portuguese immigrant in 1945, too short at the sides and greasy on top. His forearms looked like Popeye's. His hands were too small for those arms. I tried to dredge up memories of my working-class past. I always do in these places, makes it easier to communicate with the help. But that strategy was wrong here. Weldon was another type. Remember the hippies who left the city to become farmers? A simpler life, pastoral bliss, blah blah blah? Weldon was, in a way, their kindred spirit. One look told me that he had probably been a grad student at Cal. Tattoos, American cars, Betty Paige. His interest in these things started with a strong sense of irony. After awhile, he began to long for the old days that never were. Decided to work with his hands.

My romantic fantasy is the exact opposite. I spent my first years out of high school in a Sears warehouse, hefting baby furniture into a delivery truck. Then I was a janitor, a hotel clerk, whatever. My coworkers were ignorant, ugly, slovenly, illiterate. As I toiled beside them I dreamed of cafés, French cigarettes, women dressed in black. As a bonifide prole, I have no respect for proles. And I put class-tourists like Weldon in the same category as eco-tourists. They are creeps.

This only begins to explain our mutual hatred. There was something chemical, elemental, whatever. I wanted to pick up a wrench, brain him with it, and be done with it. I'm sure he thought the same. We stood close and eyed each other.

"You need a new door. I can order one today and have it back in a couple of days."

"How much?"

"I'll write up an estimate. Have a seat and I'll be back in a minute."

Weldon returned with an estimate that was much too low. I wanted to let him know that I knew, but that would blow everything. I was supposed to think that Stephie had fixed it. Well, she had fixed something. I wasn't sure why. Weldon was smiling, above it all. Must have learned that in grad school. Fierce pride welled up inside me. I know it's a trick, you idiot. But said nothing. Playing dumb is hard sometimes.

"Thank you Weldon. This is more than fair. Are you sure it's okay?"

"Stephie is an old friend. Any friend of Stephie's. In fact, I can have it for you tonight, if you like."

I didn't need the car, this being Monday. But he seemed to want me to have it. Deciding it was part of the con, I went along.

"We can rent you a loaner, or call you a cab."

"That's okay, Weldon. I feel like walking."

It's a pretty long walk, maybe three miles. North on San Pablo to Good Vibrations, corner of Dwight. I wanted to go in but I couldn't think of an excuse. I was all stocked up on condoms, and, alas, I wasn't involved with anyone kinky. With Stephie it was all still quicksilver, melting into each other and losing identity and feeling exhausted. I thought of Dino Centro. I laughed, narrowed my eyes, and thought some more. I went inside and bought some nice oil, just for luck. For next time, or for the next person, or something. I walked up a poor section of Dwight. Some of the last unkempt Victorians in Northern California. I took in the beauty of peeling paint, uncut lawns, the ripe scent of trash uncollected. A couple was selling a few old bicycles on their lawn. They looked to be out of the Great Depression. A note on the lawns: none of them were green. Nothing, in fact, had color. The sidewalk wasn't white, it was gray. The houses were in shades of faded brown. The people also seemed gray. The white people were a little dark, the black people looked faded. It was a far cry from Telegraph Avenue, where everything seems to be in primary colors. I found it all refreshing. It was like ducking into an urban museum and discovering some early Renaissance painting. A sudden quiet.

Soon the class-tourists would discover this place, and they would lift it up. There would be a Starbuck's and a chain video store, and fat little children on their way to soccer practice. May they burn in hell.

A few blocks later Dwight got more Boho, tattoo parlors and Asian restaurants. Thankfully, it's still a little shabby at the edges. I peeked into Industrial Tattoo, to see if Lorine was there. She did mine: just three words, block letters. A poem by Guisseppe Ungeretti titled "Mattina," translated by me, from an old signed edition of one of his books, found in Shakespeare & Co. in the early eighties: ENORMITY ILLUMINES ME. Down the inside of my right arm. Lorine was in the back taking a break. She had shaved her head, showing a tattoo that looked like the top of a (her?) skull.

"Hi Lorine. I like your skull."

"Great, huh? If I get sick of it I just let my hair grow back. No tattoo. Except for the nineteen others." She was wearing a t-shirt with the sleeves torn off. I could see that a short-sleeved shirt would cover the dragons, spiders, and panthers that covered her square, sturdy body. I liked that. There are times when looking normal is the best revenge. Element of surprise.

"This guy named Weldon is doing some body work on my car. Lots of tattoos. Do you know him?"

"Be careful with him. He has a temper. Reed did some stuff for him. He didn't like it and he had a hissy fit. It was great work too. He comes on all intellectual, then he wants to fight. Psycho."

I walked up to Fred's Market and got Lorine a Coke. She started in on her girlfriend problems. I tried to follow, but it was hard to put names to faces. And there were lots of names. So I nodded a lot and tried to look understanding. Finally we finished our Cokes and I made my way back to the Chandler.

The cat looked fine but I decided to take her to the vet the next day. She probably needed her shots. I called the body shop. Somebody said that the car would be finished in a couple of hours. Record time for body work. Jobs like this can take a few days. Something was up. Perhaps they wanted me to stay home? No, doesn't make sense. Lack of a car doesn't insure that in the Bay Area. There's still BART and AC Transit. Perhaps they wanted to plant something on me. But it would be tough to frame me for Peggy's murder. No motive.

I went up to the roof to get some sun. I was struck with a memory. Early in my friendship (affair? whatever) with Peggy we came upstairs on a blustery day. Nothing special happened. But I remembered her hair being ruffled by the wind, and the way she leaned over the fire escape to look at the garden that fronts the sushi place down below. Had Peggy died of natural causes this would have been a wistful, sad memory. The fact that she was murdered made these feelings unbearable. There would be sleepless nights for many years to come. Lots of nightmares. No therapist can help with this type of grief. I went back downstairs and waited in my room.

I wanted to read the old poets. I read some Thomas Carew and some Richard Lovelace. Finally I decided on an old anthology of Troubadour poetry. Poems from the days when poets could beat people up. And did. I had a feeling that I'd have to defend myself soon. Dark thoughts.

The time came to pick up my car. I decided to call Friendly Cab. The service is terrible. Often the bus is faster. But I wanted to be alone in the backseat of a car. The turbaned driver rang my bell and we sped down Haste Street until we hit rush hour traffic at Shattuck. The driver had a foul mouth for a Sikh. I found that amusing, but he felt obligated to apologize for every "fuck," addressing me as boss.

The body shop was an anti-climax. Weldon wasn't even there. The door looked great. My next step would be a visit to Earl Sheib for a paint job. I wrote a check and drove back to the Chandler. I did notice that the door felt different, but I guess that was to be expected. It was a little heavier, and the window was easier to work.

18.

I decided to finish the day with some errands. First the cat. I parked in the loading zone and put Emily in the cardboard case that I'd picked up a few days before. It was decorated to look like a circus cage. I made jokes about taking her to the circus to see the lions. Emily didn't appreciate the joke. She gave me a good scratch as I loaded her into the carrier.

By the time I got to the car she'd practically destroyed her new circus cage. She was also screaming loudly and hurling her body from one side of the cage to the other. The car door was a struggle. I fumbled with my keys as the carrier swayed with her weight. I was approached by Bruce, one of the local crazies. Remember that bald guy that was in all the John Ford movies? The one who talked real slow and had a sincere look in his eyes, even when muttering non sequiturs. I think his name was Arthur Shields. Bruce is Arthur Shields reincarnated. He stood close and stared.

"Hi Bruce." Very long pause.

"Would you like some help?"

"Yes."

"Five dollars?"

"One dollar."

"Okay."

He helped me get Emily into the passenger's seat. I fished a dollar out of my pocket.

"I said five."

"I said one." Long pause.

"Okay."

I got into the driver's side. Bruce slammed the door. Too hard. It made a weird double clunk. Something in the bowels of the door had fallen over. I didn't pay too much attention.

As I put the Miata in gear Emily popped out of the carrier and bounded into the back seat. Luckily the top was up. Otherwise she'd have joined the walking wounded at the corner of Telegraph and Dwight. Another Berkeley runaway. I threw the useless cage into the back seat and drove up to College, then right toward the Claremont Pet Hospital. I knew they'd administer the shots without an appointment, and give her a quick look-see. Emily screamed and jumped from seat to seat until we were almost there. At some point she became fixated on a strange bulge that had appeared in the upholstery of my new door. It was a hard little edge. Emily batted at it, then rubbed her lip on it, leaving a trail of cat drool. When I pulled in at the cat hospital I reached over and felt at the lump in the door. Something hard.

When we got in the waiting room Emily attacked a border collie, who then peed on the floor. I was warned against bringing her in unpacked. I promised to get a regulation cat carrier before my next visit. She was pronounced in good health and we were sent on our way. There was more screeching on the ride home. Finally I deposited her at the Chandler, where she happily ate about a pound of kibble.

I called Marvin to make sure he was home. He was, so I got back in the Miata, which was parked in a yellow zone, and drove to North Berkeley. He was in his garage when I arrived. We poked at the door. Loose part? What part would a door have? Marvin suggested that I take it back to Weldon, but I declined. There was something funny going on.

I became too curious. I had to see what was inside the door. I knocked at and around it. Hollow. But aren't these doors kind of hollow anyway? I noticed differences in the doors. The new door was heavier. I slammed them both. The new door didn't sound right. I felt a wave of frustration. Something was inside that door.

Keats said that a poet's life is one of continual allegory. I am a poet. I'm not at the level of Keats or Stein or even Tim Dlugos, but I walk the same path. And I believe that my life is a kind of symbolic narration that holds clues to the secret meanings of things. Most people choose not to pick up on these clues. Bully for them. But those who take the time to study the lives of the poets can learn something valuable.

People often ask me if I've studied Zen. I haven't. But I must have that way about me. I am, up to a point, a very patient man. Marvin says that I have the longest, slowest fuse of anyone he's ever met. Often, I'm so caught up in being amused and/or bemused that I don't notice that I'm irritated. At least not for a long, long time.

I sat on a stool in Marvin's garage. It's the kind of black, rolling stool that you see in bookstores. The staff at Moe's gave it to him when they bought some new ones. It's pretty scuffed up. I stared at the car and I thought about the door. And I thought about Maria, my ex-wife, and the rides we'd take in the Miata when it was new. In the summer we'd go down the coast almost every weekend. I thought of Maria's long, blue-black hair. Thought of her olive skin, how it became more olive as summer wore on. I remembered driving all the way to Zuma Beach one Sunday without a plan, sleeping in the car then driving back.

Marvin went into the house and came back with two Bohemia beers.

"What are you going to do?"

"There's something inside that door."

"I know, Clay. I could probably find somebody who knows how to take the door off, or how to remove the upholstery without ruining anything."

I didn't hear him, really. I walked over to the corner that holds the tools. There aren't many. Most of the garage is used for book storage. There was a mallet, a handsaw, a small shovel, and a huge pair of shears. All a little rusty. Marvin isn't much of a gardener. He lets things grow over till the neighbors complain. Then he hires somebody to cut it all back.

But there they were. A pair of oversized shears. I opened the door. I inserted the open end of the shears into the edge of the fake leather, then I ripped open the inside of the door. I cut, sawed, and chopped. After a long thoughtful silence, I had allowed my frustration to get the better of me. I 'd become rash and destructive. I had made a mess. Life as allegory.

Marvin is addicted to spectacle, especially if it involves the destruction of property. He whooped and laughed. He slammed his fist on the hood of the car. This egged me on. I tore through a couple of layers of fabric. It wasn't easy. The shears were dull and the cloth was tough. Finally I ripped away the final layer, exposing a hollowed-out door containing three brown bags tied with twine. Marvin came around to see. We stared for a few seconds at the bags. Then I grabbed one and he grabbed two. We gently put them on the hood of the car. I opened the first. Foil, then plastic, then cash. We quickly counted the bundles. One hundred hundreds, and a thousand more in smaller bills. The second bag was well padded. Bubble wrap, then a Wells Fargo check box. Weird stuff inside. Old knives and two-pronged forks. Trinkets. Something scythe-like. A strigil? But I'd imagined those to be bigger. The third package was even more padded, with bubble wrap and old newspapers. Layer after layer. Then a cheap metal box, no lock. More padding, then Dino's ultimate trinket. The Oriana Fallaci, as we'd dubbed it. About a foot tall. Smooth to the touch. Wearing a long dress and a pointed cap. Facial features smoothed by time, but there. Deep set eyes and a pointy nose. Her thin arms spread wide, like a lounge singer holding that final sentimental note.

"She's probably worth something. If you can find a fence."

"Maybe Dino will help me."

"You trust that jerk?"

We brought the stuff into Marvin's house and called Pizza Rustica. I felt strange paying with one of the twenties, but that didn't stop me. I was determined to keep that money. Better me than Weldon and Co.

Marvin cleared the table of the usual clutter and opened a bottle of Sangiovese. Oriana was standing next to the pizza, gesturing, as if to say, "Mangia, Mangia!" He was a little too happy to mention that Stephie Hearn had set me up. Hart had parked in her driveway so that I would park on the street. Wendell, or Trak, or somebody had sideswiped the Miata in the middle of the night.

"I smoked pot. I never smoked pot. I don't remember a thing."

"Probably more than pot. The bitch probably slipped you a Mickey Finn, as they say in the gangster movies."

"Maybe. I was still groggy the next morning."

"And open to suggestion. You went straight to her body guy, and he loaded the car with loot. What now?"

"According to Dino the statue is to be sold in Mexico in a few days. One possibility is that Weldon, or somebody, will try and steal the Miata tonight. They know my habit of not driving much early in the week. They could take it to Mexico and dump it before anybody notices. Or perhaps they were going to try and talk me into taking a drive down there myself. Given the right incentive, say, a library in San Diego and a night partying on the beach, I'd be up for it. And if they offered me expenses and a fee, I'd gladly drive further south. If the stuff was discovered in my car, they could play dumb."

"Who all do you think they are?"

"Hart, Weldon, Stephie, Trak. I don't think Peggy was involved."

"You don't want to."

"I'd rather not. Although she probably had possession of Oriana. That's what got her killed. But I don't think she knew what it's worth."

"What is it worth?"

"Lots, according to Dino."

"Dino and Hart could be in cahoots."

"Instincts tell me otherwise."

"Or sentiment."

"Not sentiment."

"We all get sentimental toward those we've fucked. Human nature. We don't want to believe that we were intimate with someone who is evil. Why do you think people go back to abusive lovers?"

"I'm just not that sentimental."

"Uh-huh."

19.

I have a place where I can hide things. A strange little false closet below one of the kitchen cabinets. I discovered it when I moved in. I was lining the shelves and the floor felt kind of hollow. Trap door. When covered with pots, pans and whatever it's perfectly safe. Down went Oriana, the trinkets, and some of the money. I checked my messages. Two from Hart. He had, he said, a modest proposal. Would I like to go down to Mexico with him, expenses paid? My hunches had been right.

I had parked the Miata a couple of miles away. I didn't want it stolen while I was stashing the loot. I walked down past Shattuck Avenue and got in. The car was a mess. We'd ripped up most of the upholstery, hoping to find something else, or maybe a clue. No luck. I drove to Alameda.

It was too early to do what I needed to do. I went to a Creole place called the Commodore that overlooks the yacht harbor. I ordered the Satchmo Special, red beans and rice with sausage, and a Rolling Rock. I silently toasted my ex wife, Maria, now living in New Orleans. I ate very slowly, watching the boats come and go in the early evening. It occurred to me that I might have been followed, but I pushed that worry out of my brain. I'd done enough to cover my tracks. Hart's phone messages seemed to indicate that he was clueless. I wondered if they were planning to kill me once they got the loot over the border.

I ordered peach cobbler and coffee and sat for another hour or so, watching the boats. The chef, one Frank Faté, ambled over and asked me if the food was ok. I gave him my compliments and asked for more coffee. The dinner crowd was dwindling, except for a table of eight across the room, a birthday party. They were ordering more Hennesseys as I got up to go. It was about ten.

It was warm so I put the top down. I wanted to enjoy every mile of this ride. My little Miata's last stand. I got on the freeway, over the bridge and out to Highway 1. I wanted to do the whole drive down the coast. I remembered the day we bought the car. I was skeptical and made jokes about it all, but Maria was so excited that I couldn't help feeling excited too. We went out for rides every night. We were embarrassed to be so in love with such a silly car. It wasn't, after all, a Triumph or a Sunbeam. It was a fake facsimile of those great cars of the sixties. Still, it was fun to drive. We'd put the top down, even when it was too cold. We'd go up to Grizzly Peak or into Tilden Park and make love, Maria straddling me in the passenger's seat. The high point of our short marriage.

My generation loves toys. We've sold out for them. And

I'm guilty too. For our love of toys we will someday devour the world. It's a terrible addiction with no way out. If we stop buying them now the economy will crash. If we continue, we will use up our energy sources and foul the air and water. These thoughts went through my head as I shifted into fifth and stepped on the gas. A nice sexy feeling.

For once it wasn't foggy as I approached Santa Cruz. I stopped at a café downtown for an espresso. I walked around to stretch my legs, then I got back on the highway. Monterey was also pretty warm. The air smelled salty, and it had that midsummer feel. It was around midnight and there wasn't much traffic at all. I breezed through Carmel, and then I entered the Big Sur area. I felt that fun scary feeling, like the first dip in a roller coaster. I drove fast, but not too fast. If by chance there was a witness, I wanted them to say that I was driving a little too fast. Not erratic, like a drunk driver, just a little fast. I hit a little patch of fog. Visibility went down near zero. I stepped on the gas. Plowed through the mist and hit warm air again, almost missing a turn. That might have been the end. Mr. Poet's wild ride!

I came to one of those postcard bridges. Stopped mid-bridge to look at the moon. Nobody on the road for miles, full moon, crash of the waves way down below. I wondered where Lawrence Ferlinghetti's cabin might be. Thought of Henry Miller and Jack Kerouac. Who doesn't, when in Big Sur? I thought about giving up on this plan and going to Nepenthe for a couple of Negronis. But that wouldn't do. I had to get rid of the car. Had to destroy it, actually. I didn't want somebody like Weldon inspecting the remains.

Into the car and on to the next bridge, which was the right bridge. There was a little service road just to the right

of the bridge named Pacific Street. Street sign and everything. Between the turnoff and the bridge some missing
railing. Just enough room for a Miata to go over the side
and fly. A long, dark drop. I wasn't sure if the car would
hit ocean or rock. Either would do. The tank was half full.
Hopefully that gas would blow.

I drove up to the turnoff, pulled over, and inspected the
sight. The piece of railing had been missing for all the
twenty years that I'd been doing the drive. I looked up and
down the street. No cars. I walked out to the middle of the
bridge. No traffic for a couple of miles, at least. I looked at
the drop. Was that water down there? Too dark to tell.
Fear came over me. I shivered and got back into the car.
I made one pass, but I didn't have the angle right. I made
a three-point turn, got back into position and tried again.
Couldn't do it that time either. Lost my nerve. C'mon,
Clay. They do it in the movies. You'll have plenty of time
to jump out.

I sat in the car for a good fifteen minutes. Still no traffic. I needed to get it over with. I'd left a couple of tapes in
the car for the trip down. I found an old Clash tape and I
turned it up loud. I did another three-point turn and drove
a mile or so away from the bridge, then I turned it around
again, tape so loud that it distorted. I gunned the engine a
few times and put it in gear. As I approached the spot I
opened the door. I hit it a little too fast. I jumped and
rolled, like you're supposed too, but I missed the soft sand
that I'd chosen as a target. My left arm and leg hit asphalt.
Hurt like shit, even through leather jacket and jeans. I
heard crash sounds. Adrenalin forced me back up into a
standing position. I ran to the railing with a terrific pain in
my side. The car had taken a beautiful, long fall. I listened
for motor sounds, but it was too far down. I imagined that

I heard the Clash tape. Did I? Doubt it. I strained my eyes but I couldn't see too much. Then, after a few minutes, there was an explosion, but far away. I saw a little toy flame engulf a matchbox car, way down on the rocks.

I sat propped against the railing and took a physical inventory. My jeans were ripped but there wasn't much blood. My ribs felt a little bruised but not broken. I could move my arm. The mission was a success.

My rescue came more quickly than expected. A young man shone a flashlight in my eyes, then apologized. He was with a woman. Turn-of-this-century versions of Big Sur hippies. Ash-blonde dreads and baggy clothes. Strong scent of herb. I could do worse, I thought.

"Where'd you guys come from?"

"We live down on Pac Street. Are you okay?"

"I'm not sure. I lost control of my car."

"It's gone now, brother. Hope it was insured. Can you walk?"

I got up, a little unsteady. Hippie girl helped me stay up. Strong kid. She hid her hand inside her sweatshirt and used it to wipe some dirt from my face. She had big, pothead eyes. Life is good, I thought.

They led me down the road to their cabin. It was surprisingly tidy, especially considering the many dogs and cats that came to greet me, one by one. Russ and Gail introduced me to their menagerie. Some of the animals had biblical names, which I attributed to some Rastafarian influence. Others had names that, I suppose, sound good to the hippie ear. Zafari, Aziz, Rosalia.

They gave me some herb concoction for my various scrapes and bruises. I was informed that I could stay with them until I got better, or I could call a friend. But I was not to call the cops. I figured they were somehow involved in the pot industry. Fine with me, I said. I suggested that I spend the night, then hitch a ride to the nearest pay phone. I'd tell the cops that I spent the night by the side of the road, then walked to a phone. Worked for Teddy Kennedy, why not me?

I got comfortable on the couch and heard their life story. They made it through high school in the Midwest, then came out together to escape Babylon. Five blissful years in the cabin, with occasional "business" trips. Not a bad life.

They brought out some of their products and we smoked. They treated me to their homemade dark ale. I found their singsong voices relaxing. I'm an old punk. I shaved my head in the late seventies, took lots of meth, listened to the hardest and fastest music I could find. Hated hippies. Too old to care about those differences now. Anybody who stays outside the mainstream is OK by me.

The ale and the drug took hold and I got sleepy. They brought me a sleeping bag and I fell asleep on the floor, flanked by a huge red mongrel and two black cats.

20.

It went OK with the cops. I guess I was going a little too fast, officer. I lost control. One beer, officer, but that was a couple of hours before I got in the car. It went through my mind that they might want to do a blood alcohol test. They didn't, thank goodness. Russ and Gail had been generous with the dark ale and pot. I was a little hung over.

After a morning of filling out reports and making calls they took me to Nepenthe, where I called Marvin. He told me that it would be at least three hours. Fine with me. The place is expensive, but the food is good and the view is perfect. I sat on their back patio, facing the Pacific Ocean. Warm, clear day. I won't even try to describe the beauty of that stretch of coast. I treated myself to a rare morning Bloody Mary followed by a big breakfast.

I eavesdropped on a couple who had just been to some Esalen workshops. I feel this, I feel that. I hear you, yes. I hear what you are saying. Eventually my attention was diverted by two German women. They were kissing and feeding each other sips of a Ramos Gin Fizz. I wanted to listen, but they were speaking German, so all I caught was German German haha German German Ramos Jeen Fiss! followed by a long tonguey kiss.

My thoughts turned to the caper. I had to convince Stephie & Co. that I'd gone on a little midnight ride, and accidentally put the Miata in the wide blue Pacific. They had to believe that the Oriana and the loot had gone up in flames. I needed to pull off the I, Claudius of all time. And I had to trust that Dino Centro wasn't in cahoots with them. I needed Dino to complete my plan.

I finished my breakfast and took a stroll around the gift shop. Lots of redwood burl, individualized coffee mugs, funny cards. I walked over to the observation deck and found a seat away from the ocean. The land was that California gold color, the color of dead weeds. Pretty, though. I ordered a house coffee and took in the sun until Marvin arrived.

"How'd it go?"

"I wrecked the car."

"As planned."

"It was more of an obstacle course than I'd remembered. I couldn't just roll it over the side. I had to drive and steer, and take it up over a sidewalk, then jump out."

"You should have hired a stunt man. Did it hurt?"

"Scrapes."

"No more Miata. The last souvenir. Think you'll ever see Maria again?"

I said no but I thought yes. I always see everybody again. Some karmic law, I guess. Someday when I least expect it Maria will appear. Hopefully not this year.

I slept for most of the drive up. Needed it. Marvin took me home to change and feed the cat, then over to a car rental place on Oxford Street. They put me in a sky blue Neon. I followed him back to his place and told him my exciting story. We tinkered a little with my plan and we ate lunch. He wished me luck with a bear hug, and I got into my very clean car.

I drove slowly up to Montclair but not by choice. The Neon had very little pickup. Big black SUVs flew by or tailgated. Some honked. I couldn't do much about it. I chugged along at fifty-five, then fifty, just for spite. I wasn't in a hurry to play my scene at Stephie's. I put on the radio and got come punk on KALX. I turned it up, then slowed down to forty-five. I never thought that going slow could be such an act of rebellion. I moved over to the fast lane. More honking and lots of red faces. I started to worry about being pulled over, or shot, so I zagged back to the slow lane. But it was fun while it lasted.

There was an old Mustang in the driveway, and behind that was Hart's monster SUV. They were all there. I'd have to walk into the gang headquarters and lie my head off. I collected my thoughts, walked up the long drive. I felt a cold sweat coming on. I could use that to good effect. I knocked.

Stephie answered the door and I made my entrance like Scarlet O'Hara. I found the big white couch and I collapsed. I put my arm over my face and faked a sob.

"Clay! What's wrong?"

"I wrecked the Miata."

There was a long pause. I heard the others come in. I looked up to see Hart, Weldon, and Trak. I could have guessed that the Mustang belonged to Weldon. I felt a wave of anger. These assholes wanted to use me as a mule, then kill me. I tried to use the emotion the way an actor would. I let out another good sob. Tears came to my eyes.

"You know how I like to drive down Highway 1. I went down last night. Somehow I lost control and put it over one of the big bridges. I don't know how I managed to jump out before it went. I spent the night by the side of the road. I think I'm still in shock or something."

I took my arm away from my eyes and I gave Stephie a long, soulful look. She tried to return it, but she couldn't pull it off. The color had gone out of her face. She mumbled something like, That's terrible, Clay, but there was nothing behind it. I gave her a puzzled look, and she looked away. I knew I had the upper hand, but I couldn't let that show. She got up and went to the kitchen. Came back with a glass of water. She was doing her best to keep up the con.

"Are you hurt?"

"Cuts and bruises. Nothing much. But the car is gone. It hit the rocks and it blew up. Must have burned for hours. There's nothing left. I can't believe it happened. I'm so used to that road. Maybe the steering went. I just lost control."

I sat up and I looked at them. Hart's a lousy actor. He shifted around and tried to avoid my eyes. Weldon was directing disgusted looks at Hart. Loading up my car

must have been Hart's idea. I got up and walked over to
a window.

"I'm still pretty shaky. Can I stay here for a while?"

This struck a nerve with Weldon, as I thought it would.
My hunch was that he was fucking Stephie. I had to get
my digs in. Looking back, that was a dumb thing to do. But
as I said, I had this visceral hatred of the man. I wanted to
fuck with him in the worst way.

He stepped toward me then he turned on his heels and
went to the kitchen. I tried to look innocent and dumb. He
came back with a beer, looking sullen. I looked over at
Stephie with big cow eyes. I didn't think she'd want me
around. I wanted to see how she'd get out of it.

"It's a bad time, Clay. We've got some business things
we're discussing."

"I won't be any trouble. I'm just so upset. Can't you
spare a beer?" I was probably pushing it now. I asked
myself how I'd really act if this hadn't been a setup. If it'd
all been an accident and these were really my friends. Of
course I'd want to stay and have some company.

She turned to Weldon, said, "Weldon, get him a beer."
She was a little short.

Weldon gave her a look that could kill, then, without
softening, looked at me. But he did get me the beer. He
handed me the beer and I came very close to blowing it.
He wasn't really any more hateful than the rest. But that
deep chemical hatred filled me with adrenalin. I wanted to
grab the bottle, beat him to death with it, and get it all over
with. I searched my brain for an image that would calm
me. And all I came up with was the last scene in *The Wild
Bunch*, that beautiful moment when the Bunch, though
outnumbered, start the shooting. I replayed the scene, and
it felt like a delicious temptation. But I also saw it as a cau-

tionary tale. I wasn't ready to make that suicidal move.

I slowly drank my beer. I told them to go on with their business, that it wouldn't bother me. Hart made something up about his poetry fantasy camp. The conversation kept dwindling. I asked him about Pinsky. He said that Pinsky had dropped out, but that he could get Creeley, if he could come up with the money. He had Wanda Coleman, Dorianne Laux, and David Bromige. He just needed one big star to bring the students down. As he spoke his voice trailed away, mid-sentence. Everybody looked in opposite directions and waited for a chance to go. Like small talk at a funeral.

I decided to go and leave them to discuss my fate. My sense was that they had believed me. I suppose, if they didn't, they could have killed me then and there. But they didn't make a move. Stephie gave me a cold hug, the best she could manage. I held onto her for a couple of extra seconds, then kissed her on the lips. Looked over her shoulder at Weldon. He looked away.

Out to the Neon and then down to Berkeley Bowl for a piece of salmon. I owed Marvin a good dinner. Berkeley Bowl was pandemonium. I noticed, standing in line, that I had the most normal hairstyle in the store. Mine is brown and short. Theirs was green, bleached white, stringy, shaved, sticking straight up. You don't see hair like theirs on the evening news. With a hairdo like that, I thought, looking at a late-seventies style Mohawk, you can't run for congress. Every so often I'm reminded that Berkeley is still rather strange. It makes my day.

The traffic, alas, was also typically Berkeley. I circled People's Park eight times, going west as far as Shattuck, turning left, then heading up Dwight toward the hills. Finally a tiny place opened up on Haste, in front of a free box. A grizzled wino type was standing in the middle of the pile, shopping for a shirt. He tried on a pink one with a V-neck, but that didn't do. The frilly white blouse was too small. He decided on a steel blue T that loudly advertised Merrill Lynch, then waded out of the pile and thrust both fists upward in a victory salute.

I had barely finished slicing the tomatoes and mozzarella when Marvin arrived. In honor of the warm weather I made a pitcher of lemonade, spiked with vodka. Marvin tore into the bread and tomatoes with barely a hello.

"They're going to come after you."

"No. I don't think so. I think I snowed 'em."

"Don't be surprised if you're apartment gets turned upside down."

"No, no. Really. They believed me." Marvin had a way of eroding my confidence.

"Okay. They believed you. Where do you go from here?"

I unveiled my plan as we ate a long, slow dinner. I was careful to offer him a good cut of the loot. I slowly increased his cut whenever he registered a complaint. By the end of the evening he was on board at fifty-fifty.

21.

I went over to Bongo Burgers and ordered a Persian Burger. While I was waiting I set up a dummy e-mail account at Streetspace, one of those email stations that have appeared in public spaces. Username: makedinorich.

I emailed Dino and told him that I had something he would be interested in. He could probably track me down through some electronic means that I don't understand. But it didn't matter much. I really wanted to give him plausible deniability in the event that Hart and the gang questioned him. It did occur to me that he might be loyal to them, but I decided to take a chance that he wasn't. He'd want the loot for himself.

I was a little anxious. I checked my e-mail from home after dinner. Nothing. I went down to Moe's to browse. I hadn't been buying and selling many books lately. I found an old out-of print-book by Harold Norse. I had a trade slip in my wallet somewhere. Moe's issues trade for books, as well as paying cash. I usually keep a trade tab going. I searched my wallet, but I couldn't find it. I had one of the found hundreds in my pocket so I broke it. This loot wasn't going to last. I wondered if the cash could be traced back directly to Thomas. The missing cash that got me into this mess. Oh well, money is money.

Moe's has a free e-mail machine, identical to the one in Bongo Burgers. It's located in the Critical Theory section. I decided to try my luck. I stood at the machine, which resembles something that you might see on the Starship Enterprise. Most contemporary design is based on Star Trek, or some other bad TV show. We're the generation that couldn't grow up. As I logged on I became aware that the works of Theodore Adorno and Walter Benjamin were looking over my shoulder. Sorry, guys. The screen treated me to a series of ads. It played some space-age music (Adorno had a problem with jazz. What would he think of this?) then it allowed me to see my mail.

Dino had also set up a dummy account, under the username figaro. I wondered if he was up at Bongo Burger, picking up a Persian Burger. More likely he was at Café Roma. Our stupid lives. His was a simple message: show me some proof and I'll get back to you.

I went back to the Chandler. I opened a Bohemia and leafed through the Norse book:

> I was made to be a hero
> but there were no causes
> & besides I was too short.

I pulled the stuff out of the false-bottomed cupboard. I selected a trinket. I didn't know what it was. A butter knife with a hole cut out of the blade. A bottle opener, before the days of screwtops? Something for cake decoration? Funny, Clay. I'll probably never know. It fit nicely into a small size manila envelope. On the envelope I scrawled I'VE GOT THE STATUE. I slipped it into a Moe's bag along with a book for ballast. I left Oriana out on the kitchen table while I drank and read poetry. She was beautiful, really. That ancient, quiet feeling came over me, like what you feel when you visit the Coliseum or the Parthenon. I had one of those when-this-is-all-over thoughts. When this is all over, I'll go to Rome for a month or two. I've got a good pile of money, with possibly more to come. I dreamed of Italy. I looked Oriana in her buggy eyes. Are you going to lead me to an apartment on the Spanish Stairs? I wondered why anyone would want her so badly. If I may look for you without offense/I beg you, darling, where's your hiding place? Except that her hunter(s) had committed great offense.

I finished the Bohemia and took the stuff over to Shakespeare & Co. They know me, so they don't ask to me to check my bag at the door. I went back to the literature section and I located a copy of Mann's *Joseph the Provider*. You will find a copy in every used bookstore in the English-speaking world. And probably in Germany, too, come to think of it. It is also a book that never sells. I took it off the shelf, and I pulled out the artifact. I leaned it against the back of the case, and replaced the Thomas Mann. At some point Harvey, the owner, will sell the store. Perhaps then, during a remodel, someone might disturb *Joseph the Provider*. My package was safe.

I walked back home and emailed figaro/Dino. I went to the YMCA and got a little exercise, then I did some writing, ate dinner, watched the news. Checked the mail around eleven. No answer.

There was a message the next morning. The piece was authentic. He wanted to see "the girl." There was only one buyer. This person had a sentimental attachment to her, and he would consider paying a quarter of a million, which was many thousands more than the market price. He offered me a cut of one hundred thousand. And he wanted a thousand up front for expenses. I decided not to dicker. Fifty thousand to me, fifty to Marvin. Add that to the money I found in the Miata. Not a bad caper.

Arranging a drop-off was difficult. He kept rejecting my suggestions. Finally it was decided that I would go to Amoeba Records on a Saturday afternoon and check a backpack at the security counter. I would take the claim check upstairs to the classical room and leave it in the Bartok section at two o'clock sharp. He would give me five minutes to get out, retrieve the claim check, and leave with the girl. The security people wouldn't know the difference. Saturdays are busy. They wouldn't remember a face.

I entered the record store with several customers and drifted into the Saturday crowd. It was like being at a too-crowded party. I had trouble wading through the crowd to the classical section. I was getting behind schedule. I made my way upstairs to where it was less crowded. I deposited the chit in the right place. I took most of the allotted time for me to get downstairs and through the jazz section. When I hit rock n' roll I couldn't move. I saw figaro/Dino coming through the crowd. I'd taken too long. Should I play dumb?

"Hello Dino. Doing some shopping?"

"Yes. Pablo Casals. I've been looking for a certain performance."

Long pause with lots of rippling possibilities. Did he know what I knew that he knew? I decided to let it drop. Plausible deniability.

22.

I knew that I was taking a chance by letting Oriana out of my sight. It would be easy enough for Dino to disappear. I wouldn't have the resources or the inclination to hunt him down. But I wasn't too worried. I had lots of cash, more than I'd ever expected to make from this job. And he had possession of the statue. Let them tear up my apartment. They wouldn't find a thing.

I felt light and easy and it was a beautiful day. I thought I'd to go up to Tilden Park and do a little hiking, or maybe BART out to the Mission to watch the young new bohemians eat fussy food and smoke imported cigarettes. The Bay Area is rich in cheap entertainment.

I thought about it awhile, then I had a second cup of coffee. A ragged group of Hare Krishnas stopped their parade just below my window. I moved my chair over to the window to get a better look. It was a subdued group at first. Then one member, a tall, gangly young man with a skull-like head, caught the spirit, or whatever it is they catch. He had a beautiful chanting voice, and he whirled like a dervish. He lost his bearings and caromed off of a trash can and into Dwight Way, where his saffron robe caught the spokes of a student's bike. The student, a punk-ish guy in Seattle anarchy gear (big boots, baggy pants, black sweatshirt, shaved head) went down hard, but he bounced up like a fighter who'd been stunned by a left hook. The two men looked each other up and down, standing dumbly in the right hand lane. There was an apology, and Mr. Krishna resumed his chanting, dancing around the damaged bike. This caused the student to laugh hysterically. Meanwhile, traffic was backing up on Dwight Way, and horns were blowing. A crusty old homeless man, known as Pops, was annoyed by this. He attacked a classic yellow Carmen Ghia, and had to be pulled off the hood of the car by a couple of the regular denizens of the street. A few gawkers gathered. The student punk tried to shoo them away. A pushing match ensued. It was time to call the cops, but nobody called the cops. The scene just kind of played itself out. The gawkers moved away, Pops stumbled down Telegraph, yelling, Fuck you over his shoulder. The Krishnas started up their chant. It was as if someone said, Fight's over, turn up the music.

Several times a day I see a small version of the last scene of *The Day of the Locusts*. I'm thankful for that. Normal folks are still a little wary of my neighborhood. Those nuts are all that stand between me and gentrification. I poured myself another cup. Perhaps I'd stay home today and watch the world outside my window.

I put the three Rachmaninoff symphonies on the CD player and turned it up loud. They added nicely to the mood. Car horns, drums in the park, strings too romantic to be taken seriously, but then you take them seriously because life is just that overwhelming and corny. If you aren't living through holy hell or dizzying highs you aren't doing it right. A murdered friend, stolen goods, a few betrayals, three affairs. What a summer! I sat down to write a poem and things made sense, at least for the duration of the writing of the poem. Oh now it is that all this music tumbles round me which was once considered muddy.

I was sitting at my desk when Marvin called. It was getting dark. He reminded me that Creeley was reading at the University that night. I decided to go. I liked some of his early books, and it would be an interesting scene.

I had a couple of hours to kill. I made myself a Campari and orange juice and I read a little Creeley, then a little Cid Corman. Marvin came up and I made him a drink, and we walked to the UC campus.

The reading was in the Maude Fife room, on the third floor of the Wheeler Auditorium. It's a dreary building, but I believe it has some historical significance. Like much of the University it is poorly kept. I always get lost on my way to Maude Fife, but Marvin knows the way through the drab halls and stairways.

When we got there a few people were congregating in the hallway. It was a good mix of local poets and their students. Clark Coolidge was there, and Gloria Frym. I noticed Michael Palmer and Ishmael Reed. We went into the small auditorium. The lighting was bad. Institutional.

But I've always loved the chairs. They have a faux antique look. Louis the something. But I suspect that they were bought in the 70s and repainted in the 80s. The country's premier poets have read in this room. Ashbery, Rich, Dorn. Upstairs and in the back. Most people don't even know about the series. There's very little publicity. Such is poetry in America.

We took our seats, in the middle of the room. The entrance was up near the stage so we could watch people enter. Stephie Hearn entered. Alone. I was surprised to see her at a reading. She didn't see me, or pretended that she didn't . I wondered how I should play this little scene. I looked over at Marvin. He was wearing a sly smile.

And then she did see me, and I stood up and hugged her, and we sat together. Another little game of Does she know that I know what she knows?

"I didn't expect to see you here."

"But I expected to see you. I've been worried about you since the crash. Are you doing okay?"

"I guess. I miss my car. And I've had a few of those classic falling nightmares."

She paused for a while before she asked, "Were they able to recover the car?"

"No. Burned to a crisp. At some point they'll clear away the carcass. But they don't seem to be in a hurry. That's between AAA and the city."

Robert Hass stepped up to the mike, wearing a Mr. Rogers sweater and a new agey grin. He happy-talked an intro to the opening act, a third-generation language poet, and a grad student at the university. She looked like the book clerk Bogey flirted with in *The Big Sleep*. Blonde hair in a bun and a sensible dress. She would set up each poem with a breathy, giggly intro that was sly and funny.

Then she'd switch into her poetry voice: serious, plodding, awful. The strings of pointless words put me into a semi-stupor. Marvin started to giggle. He leaned over and said, "Not a decent . . ." which is one of our inside jokes, a reference to a William S. Burroughs line from the sixties: "Not a decent fuck in the entire generation."

She had the presence of mind to cut it short. She knew she was only the opening act. Smattering of applause. Hass came out and announced that there'd be no break. My heart sank. I knew that several bottles of good wine were waiting in the classroom that doubles as a reception space. I was hoping to grab a glass between acts. I don't remember a word of the intro to Creeley, but I do recall that Hass' eyes glistened with tears of sincerity.

Creeley sounded beautiful, and he read enough of his old poems to make me feel nostalgic, and to remind me why I took up poetry. His late work is too warm and fuzzy, even if it does deal with death. He's much loved, which is deadly to anyone in the arts. Still, who doesn't long to be loved? Can't hardly blame him. Some poets age well (Harold Norse, Barbara Guest, Carl Rakosi), others get cute. It occurred to me that a Robert Creeley reading is like a Moody Blues concert. You go to hear the hits.

He finished his reading to loud, long applause and was mobbed as he left the podium. Hass announced the number of the wine room. Marvin bolted for the door. I hoped he'd score me a glass of red. Stephie said she'd come to the reception. She wanted to tell Creeley that Hart said hello.

"Where is Hart?"

"Down in Mexico with Weldon. They're still trying to put together the workshop."

"Is Creeley going down?"

"Yes, but not for the whole six weeks. He'll do a reading and a one-day workshop. Hart had to cut down on expenses."

"Who else did he get?"

"Jack Gilbert, possibly Carolyn Kizer."

Definitely second-tier poets, I thought. Hart must be having a cash flow problem about now. I started to feel a little pissed that he didn't invite me, even though I'm really about a fourth-tier poet. Then I remembered the situation.

We waded through the hallway with the crowd. There was much hobnobbing and handshaking. In that close quarters I was reminded that poets often smell gamey. Too preoccupied to bathe?

The party room had the drab, undecorated look that we associate with Soviet communism. The cork bulletin boards were bare. A long table, a type that you'd remember from elementary school, was loaded with mid-priced California wines, crackers, cheese, and fruit. Another table displayed some of Creeley's books. I was taken by the gray sameness of the covers.

I became very aware of Stephie's presence as the only sexual entity in the room. Well, except Marvin, who isn't my type. The young language poet who opened the show seemed too stiff and lifeless to ever bother with anything physical. I saw her talking to an editor from UC Press, wearing a frozen smile, like someone at a wedding reception. I knew instinctively that her only concern was her career. Everyone else was busy chasing prizes or publication, or a few minutes with the star. If I walked around the room and pricked each of them with a needle, would they bleed? Poets are supposed to bleed.

I was standing next to Stephie, then she turned to speak to somebody. I turned in the other direction, to say hello to somebody else. We were back to back, then our backs touched. I started to lean away, but she leaned back. Our elbows touched, and we turned our heads until our cheeks almost touched. I felt a little light-headed. Reminded myself, again, of the situation. She possibly conspired to kill Peggy Denby. And then there was the car. Were they planning to leave me for dead on the road, once Oriana was over the border?

I couldn't sleep with her under these circumstances. Could I? She'd only sleep with me for reasons of manipulation. Perhaps she wanted to make sure that I didn't have the loot. Trick me into saying the wrong thing. The thought of that only heightened my sexual tension. Sick fuck!

I knew she wanted me. I knew from our past encounters that she was attracted to me. The sexiest lover is a willing lover. And she liked it. Most people don't. Oh, they like it once in awhile, or at the beginning of a relationship. But after that it becomes messy and troublesome. Or, for some, it's like taking a shit. Necessary to good health. For me, it is a third of my personal holy trinity: Sex, Poetry, Travel. We wouldn't agree on the other two, although she liked traveling well enough. But we both treated sex as a first priority. No, not just that. A sacred thing.

We left Marvin at the party. He interrupted his diatribe on politics and poetry long enough to give me a look that could kill. I shrugged, and we went out into the night, up

Telegraph toward my apartment. It was a warm, noisy September evening. Students and homeless people stood in clumps, blocking our path. Food, wrappers, and an occasional supine body littered the Avenue. The younger ones hadn't yet learned to clean up after themselves.

We entered the Chandler and took the elevator to the fourth floor. Emily greeted me with a cry for food. Stephie was indifferent toward her. But the sight of Peggy's cat made me feel creepy. I decided that I'd betray my religion that night.

"Can I have one of your famous Negronis?"

"Of course." I went into the kitchen and started to arrange drinks. She followed me in and stood very close. She bumped me once, then again. She sighed the word "Warm," wiped her brow, then took off her shirt, revealing a men's black sleeveless T, cut very short. She looked a little boyish, with her short hair and muscled shoulders. She was naturally beautiful, and she was rich enough to enhance that beauty: personal trainers, beauty products, great clothes. A walking airbrushed model. I shouldn't be attracted to this type, but I am. I don't like them. They're barely human, put on this earth to consume, which keeps our economy afloat. Over the years they have made their way as ad executives, agents, personal finance consultants, magazine editors, realtors. These days they are the e-people, buying and selling junk text and bad graphics through high-speed phone lines.

She had the finest lines I've ever seen on a woman. It occurred to me that Dino Centro had the finest lines of any man. I'd been living in a sexual Xanadu all summer long. Had that corrupted me? I tried to focus on that thought. Why were these unscrupulous people so interesting? Marvin, with his puritanical streak, would see the failure of communism in this. I remembered a story about Mayakovsky buying an expensive car (a Bugatti?) when he was sent to Paris in the twenties, angering the stuffy party types.

It occurred to me that I was aroused by her possible involvement in the murder. This thought put my brain into one of those repulsion/attraction spins that can, at times, heighten awareness very much like an amphetamine high. I gulped my drink and tried to pull myself together.

She finished her Negroni, and poured the rest of the pitcher into her glass. The bartender in me winced. Negronis should be made one at a time. The dregs are too watery. I pointed this out.

"I don't give a fuck. I'm lushing it up tonight." She pulled a chair from the kitchen table and swung it around backwards, and sat that way, her legs spread in tight jeans. It was a corny move, coquettish in a bad movie way. I loved it. "Tell me what happened when your car went over the cliff," she said.

"Why do you want to know?"

"It must have been a thrill, in a way. I mean, since everything turned out all right. Don't you think back on it as kind of exciting?"

"No, I was too scared." I made a quick mental review of my story. I couldn't afford to get caught in a lie.

"Did you see the car fall? Like in the movies?"

"I was too stunned. But I did hear explosions. The car hit the beach instead of the water. It burned to a crisp on the sand."

She waved her glass, demanding a refill. "Did the cops find you?"

I refilled the pitcher with new ice and stirred a new drink. "No, Steph, didn't I tell you? I passed out for a few hours, then I walked back to the police station." I wondered if she caught my nervousness. I'm a good liar, but I'm not psychotic. I feel uneasy when I'm fibbing.

She got up and grabbed the pitcher from me, and she poured me a huge one. Hers was slightly smaller. She tried to make it seem like an accident. But I knew the game. She was trying to fill me full of truth serum. Refusing the drink would arouse suspicion. I had to keep my head, while losing it. Or perhaps drink her under the table. An interesting challenge. I felt a perverse excitement rise into my already fuzzy brain.

To her credit she never came on with the old, Clay, I love you, I've always loved you. She probably knew that wouldn't wash. She used her best assets. She leaned on me hard as I poured her third (fourth?) drink. She paraphrased Dorothy Parker, fake slurring: "I like Negronis, two at the most, three I'm under the table, four I'm under the host." She zigzagged to the stereo, put on the *Magnetic Fields* CD that I'd been saving for another seduction and flopped on my bed, which doubles as a couch. I naturally moved toward her, but she slowed things down with a little small talk. Something about the office, something about software. She was manipulating me, but on some level she also took this software talk seriously. I think it turned her on. Many people find the information highway, stock options, and websites sexy. It's probably a class thing. These people get off on the scent of money. It gives them their sexual thrust.

She must have noticed my glazed look. She leaned foreward and kissed me, then she backed off again. She sipped her drink and talked some more. She brought up a new TV show that was stirring up some controversy. Contestants were asked to do various degrading things.

Those that refused had to leave the show. On the thirteenth week the two finalists were taken to a beautiful home in the Hollywood Hills. In the back yard, with a view of the Capitol Records building, a thirties style swimming pool was filled with beef blood, cat urine, and dog shit. The first contestant to lap the pool won the deed to the house.

"Did you watch it last night?"

"I missed it, somehow."

"It was great! Constance won!"

"Which one was she? I only watched it a couple of times."

"Clay, you goof! How could you miss it. Constance was the lesbian therapist. Remember? She cried because the show was taking quality time away from her and her daughter."

"What about the guy with testicular cancer? I kind of liked him."

"He was a jerk. Negative and gruff. He got thrown off because he wouldn't do the naked bungee jump."

This went on for awhile. The diversions of the so-called middle class. Bored with all but the most inane trivialities, they fill up their time with this fluff. Well, me too. I know the plots of every Rocky and Bullwinkle episode, the lyrics to every Beach Boys song. Western culture really is decadent and destructive. But we're already hopelessly ruined. Perhaps we should be exterminated.

"Clay, are you listening?"

"Yes, of course. I think the Negronis stunned me."

"You haven't been the same since the accident. Why don't you talk about it?" As she said this she got up and went to the kitchen, returning with a tumbler of ice and the gin. We were getting serious.

I needed to get specific, to make the lie more plausible. "I didn't tell the cops this, Stephie, but I was reaching for a tape when I lost control of the car. I was getting a little tired. It wasn't the Miata's fault. I guess after that I panicked. The top was down, and I bailed. Man overboard! I hit a patch of gravely dirt, then I rolled back onto the pavement. I crawled around for awhile, then I propped myself up on the handrail in time to hear the explosions. I blacked out, and woke up hours later on a dirt path that leads into the woods. I tried to hitch a ride. No luck, so I walked to the station. End of story."

"Was the car driving OK?" Her voice was a little too sharp, and she knew it.

"Yes, everything seemed fine."

She seemed agitated. She poured more gin into her half finished drink, then took a healthy gulp. "It seems strange to me that you were just riding along, minding your own business and the car went into the drink."

"Actually it smashed on the rocks and sand. These things happen."

Her face took on a demonic look. I found that comical so I laughed. She took another gulp. "Something's funny, Clay. The car must have veered to the right, or something."

"No. It didn't veer at all until I lost control."

She stood up, with some effort. She went into the bathroom muttering to herself. She stayed a long time. When she came out I noticed that she'd splashed water on her face. She poured more gin into the icy water.

"Stephie, you're ruining that good gin. Would you like some fresh ice?"

More of that comical demonic look. She slowly and deliberately stood up, the tumbler in her hand. I assumed she was getting the ice. Then, with shocking force, she hurled the heavy glass at the wall, hitting my Franz Kline print (bought at MOMA during a trip to NYC) square in the middle of the blackest part. The glass didn't shatter. It broke into two or three pieces, far as I could tell. I wondered if the solid walls of the Chandler Apartments could be damaged. Probably not.

"You fucking piece of shit! You knew it was in there! They didn't want to tell me. They were trying to fuck me over. But I overheard so they cut me in. You pulled her out with your grubby little hands, then you drove off the bridge. And you hid her before you went to the cops. You idiot, you stole that story from Teddy Kennedy! It was you and Marvin, that skulking piece of commie dogshit." She grabbed the gin and took a long slug from the bottle. "I need that money. My investors are getting nervous. I have a mortgage, an office, two cars, and a couple of credit cards. I have to show a profit somewhere. I just have to."

She hung her head. It looked for a second like she was winding down. I began to search my addled brain for strategies. I expected her to melt down into tears, but she didn't. She swung the near-empty bottle of Sapphire gin. I moved in the right direction, but I was a little slow, due to the cocktails. The bottle caught me upside the head. It was only a glancing blow, but it stung. I had that feeling that you have when you're under the influence and something painful happens. I thought, Ouch, that would have hurt.

For the next several minutes she was an uncaged banshee. The gin bottle went through the living room window. I heard the crash below and scurried over to look. Luckily there wasn't much traffic on Dwight Way at that hour. I'd have to pay for the window, but that's all. She toppled the stereo speakers and a bookshelf. I did my best to stay out of the way. I had no choice but to let her rave until exhausted. I was surprised that someone on Prozac could work up so much passion. She went after the cat, but I scooped Emily up and threw her in the closet. For this I caught a palm on the ear. My hearing went funny.

"Where is she? I want the statue! They don't think you're smart enough but I know you better, you walking bag of shit!"

We know that clichés are based on a nut of truth. You're beautiful when you're angry, dear. I didn't say that out loud, but I wanted to fuck her in the worst way. It was one of those horrible moments that feminist men run into, when postmodern attitudes come up against a thousand years of conditioning (natural history?). The Taming of the Shrew.

She grabbed my copy of Lorine Niedecker's *Collected Poems* and tore the slim volume in two. But her eyes glazed over as she dropped both halves at the same time. She was losing interest in inanimate objects. I sensed that I was in trouble.

She put her arms out like two battering rams and rushed me. I took one hand in the solar plexus, the other in the chin. I went down hard, but I managed to roll to the side. I looked up as she grabbed a pair of scissors, a rather rusty old pair that I keep on my desk for no particular reason. She dropped on me, knees first, like the TV wrestlers do. She held the scissors with both hands, ready to plunge. I was a beaten man.

"Where is she?"

"I don't know what you're talking about, Stephie. You're having a bad reaction to the gin. Maybe it doesn't mix well with antidepressants."

She looked a little confused. If I could just keep up the lie for a little longer without getting killed I could find some sort of opening.

"Then who has her?"

"I don't know. I don't know who she is, or what I have to do with it. Why don't you let me up and tell me about it? Maybe I could help."

"No. You're a motherfucker. A dickweed. A walking piece of shit."

She was working herself into an even higher form of hysteria. To my relief, she threw the scissors away. They hit a bookshelf with a thunk. She straddled me, and she lowered her middle onto mine. She pulled off her shirt. She was dripping with sweat.

Although aroused, I was also understandably confused. I said, "Are we going to fuck now?" and she laughed.

"We're going to do whatever I like!"

She got up and went into the kitchen. Oh God, not more booze, I thought. I felt the fear that you feel around the truly insane. Fear mixed with fascination. She came back with a chef's knife, actually my best one. She stood, topless in jeans, glistening, butch haircut, crazed look in her eyes. She held the knife like she knew how to use it.

"I want to know where the statue is. My financial life depends on it. If you tell me, we can split the take. If you don't I'll cut off your cock and feed it to Peggy's cat. Either way you're going to fuck me first because I'm hot as hell. That is Peggy's cat, isn't it?"

"Did you kill Peggy?"

"No. Hart's boys did."

"Then you haven't killed anybody yet. Why start now?"

"Who said I haven't killed anybody?"

Even in times of great danger I'm pretty cool, so I didn't say, "Uh-Oh" out loud. But I thought it.

She told me to stand up so, of course I did. My ribs felt bruised and my left ear was throbbing. She wrapped her arms around me, holding the knife upright behind my back. I could feel the tip through my cotton T-shirt. When she kissed me she put her tongue in my mouth. I liked that. I don't always have to lead the dance. She pushed me back a little, and the knife tip gave me a good prick. I realized that this fuck could be my last. Imagine the performance anxiety!

She backed off, took off her jeans, and got on the bed. No underwear. My, how boys like that. She motioned me over with the knife, and pointed. I went down on her with the tip of the flat of the knife on the back of my head. If I moved wrong the tip would scratch the nape of my neck. She got more excited and threw her hands back over her head, still holding the knife. I thought it was an opening, and stopped for a second. But I was too slow. I looked up to see the knife an inch from my nose.

"Back to work, asshole!"

After a long while she flipped over onto her stomach. Again she was holding the knife over her head, completely stretched out. I was embarrassed to be so aroused by the situation, but at least I was aroused. I entered her from behind. As we fucked, I ran one hand up her arm, to the hand that held the knife. Every muscle in her body tightened.

"Pathetic piece of shit. Don't even try. And you keep that fuckstick fully inflated!"

She wanted me to finish with her on top, so I did, looking into her half-crazed eyes. Then she got up and sauntered into the kitchen for a glass of water. She stood in front of the broken window and drank. At that moment she was the most amazingly beautiful woman that I'd ever seen.

"Sorry about the window. I'll pay for it. Now, are we partners, or are you dead?"

She turned toward the window and looked through the broken panes. It was as if she was giving me a few minutes of privacy in which to decide my fate.

I had a second, or less, to act. I lunged at her, using the edge of the bed as a starting block. The knife clanked on the floor. She gave me a surprised look as I pushed her through what was left of the glass. There happened to be an SUV speeding up Dwight Way. She hit the ground and seconds later the car hit her.

I'd have a lot of explaining to do. But it was better then getting skewered.

24.

I've done more than my share of the police interview shuck and jive. I just don't know, officer. We only had two drinks, and without any reason she grabbed a knife and came at me. We struggled, and she fell.

They didn't believe me at first. I waived my right to a lawyer and told my story, over and over. Then, for reasons that I didn't understand, they let me go. I'd expected to spend the night. And I'd fully expected to be booked for manslaughter, probably the next day. But the cops let me off with a stern look and a Don't leave town. Of course, that didn't mean that they wouldn't book me later.

I got home at first light. A crew was still examining the scene of the crime. I called my lawyer. He made some joke about the things that happen in the sleazy quarters of the city. He said that a manslaughter trial was a possibility, but that he doubted it. There was no glory in prosecuting a case like this. We made an appointment for the following day.

I hadn't eaten but I didn't have an appetite. I waited for the last of them to leave, then I took a shower and put on some clean clothes. I went up to the roof. It was warm but autumn was coming on. The breeze from the Bay had a cool bite. It was foggy in Marin. I couldn't see Mount Tam. But San Francisco was clear and the water was a beautiful blue.

I didn't try to fight the numbness that I was feeling. Shock was the proper reaction. It keeps us from cracking up. I sat in a rusty lawn chair and stared and stared. I thought about my part-time job. It started out as a few favors for troubled friends. Then I got hooked on the danger. I came up with some phony theories about my place in this subculture. Underground detective, protector of the weak. Mensch. Can a killer be a mensch? Can a killer be a book scout? I've killed a handful of people now. Not as many as my great-uncle Eric, who flew a bomber in the Pacific. Not as many as my friends who fought in Viet Nam. Not as many as Castro, Mao, LBJ, George Bush & Co. Do numbers matter?

As I rationalized, sitting on the rusty chair, the clouds came in over the city and the water turned from blue to gray. With great effort I switched mental gears. Things were messier now. What of Weldon, Hart, and Trak? I needed to make them go away. Or slither away myself.

I went down to the basement and found some cardboard to cover the window. Took the elevator back because my legs were shaky. I'd have to call the manager soon. I'm sure he knew what happened. All the other neighbors too. And my street friends, and the buyers at Moe's. They probably wouldn't bring it up. But everyone in South Berkeley would identify me as the guy who threw a naked woman out of his window.

I finished the patch job and cleaned up some of the mess. Pulled out the espresso maker and started some coffee. There was a knock on the door and I went into a fighter's stance, like a punch-drunk boxer. It was Nellie Miles from the third floor. She's one of the really young ones who, for some reason, take me into their confidence. They seem to think I'm safe. I guess I am. I listen to their boyfriend problems. I give them beers. I guess they think I'm a nice old guy. I actually do lust after them, especially Nellie. But vanity keeps me from making advances. I imagine them saying, "Oh, gross! You're too old!" That's when I get up and take a deep breath, or wash my face, or open another beer.

Nellie was, I think, nineteen. A pretty girl with shiny light brown hair. I don't use the word girl in a derogatory way. You just wouldn't call her a woman.

She looked kind of sheepish. She giggled, then she produced a pipe. "I'm sorry about what happened. Do you need to smoke some pot?"

"Maybe a little." I appreciated the act of friendship. It was pretty courageous, considering what I'd just done.

She sat on the bed and we passed the pipe. I gave it the old President Clinton, not wanting to get too high. I had work to do.

"A reporter came around and talked to us. We said you were nice."

"He interviewed all of you?"

"A bunch of us. We were down in the lobby."

"Oh. I didn't notice. Too upset."

"You don't have to talk about it." She was giving me the once-over twice. I tried to imagine how she felt. She'd told me her life story, trusted me, and now this. Like most her age, she would find a way to turn it into her own personal tragedy.

"I probably shouldn't say much. You know, lawyers and all. But I'm not a murderer."

"Everybody's sure it was an accident. We like you. I like you. You're a good friend." She lit the pipe again. Then she sat for a few minutes, looking uncomfortable. "Should I go now? I don't want to get in the way."

"You probably should. But I appreciate your stopping by."

She stood up and put her hands behind her back. She reached her head up and kissed me on the cheek. Tears came to my eyes.

"Call me."

"I will." She walked down the hall. I watched her for a few seconds before shutting the door. I went back inside and I noticed that she'd left the pipe on the nightstand.

25.

I washed the dishes from the night before. There was a lipstick smudge on the tumbler. She took a sip from the tumbler, she said something to me, she looked out the window, then I killed her. I washed the glass. Then I washed the martini pitcher and the other glasses, and finally the chef's knife. It looked clean, but there had to be traces of blood. She'd pricked me pretty good. I'd thrown on a clean shirt before going downstairs, and I guess I didn't bleed through. Good. I didn't tell the cops about our dangerous game.

I put on one of Beethoven's late string quartets. My first instinct was to try to relax, get some sleep. But I couldn't do that. I needed to jump into all this craziness until the job, whatever that might be, was finished. So I turned the music up loud. Its complex and scary. A swan dive into the void.

My thoughts began to race and I felt twitchy. Was I up to this? I convinced myself that I was. Into the void, become the void, love the void, make the void my own. Negative capability. My mind filled with plans and alternative plans.

There was a knock on the door. Probably Nellie, back for her pipe. I didn't bother to turn down the music.

"Mr. Blackburn?"

"Yes." I'd opened the door wide. A stupid thing to do. She was a mystery-eth. Pacific Islands Anglo? African Philipino? Couldn't tell. She was quite tall. I noticed a tattoo peeking from her sleeve. If Queequeg were a woman . . . She was wearing pleated khakis, a Gap shirt, and a red scarf, badly tied. Her countenance told me that she was come kind of cop.

"I'm agent Bailey Dao, FBI."

I decided to let her in. There was nothing in the apartment that could incriminate me. Except the pipe, which I'd momentarily forgotten.

She strode in, to the middle of the room. They like to let themselves all the way in. She was square and stiff. Whatever her ethnic background, she had an Irish jaw.

I've only seen jaws like that in Ireland, and then only in the rural counties. Big, scary, farmer jaws. Somehow, a dairy farmer in Tipperary had gained entry into this stew of genes. So fitting for a cop.

"I told the Berkeley police everything I could. Who called the FBI ?"

"We're investigating a federal crime."

I shut my mouth and half closed my eyes. I couldn't allow myself to be a wise guy. I told myself that she was feeding me these easy lines, hoping for me to bite. I smiled and nodded.

"Do you know the whereabouts of Hart Denby?"

"I believe he's in Mexico."

"Where in Mexico?"

"San Felipe, I think."

"And Weldon Key?"

"I'd guess he's down there too."

She sat on the bed, trying to look casual. She looked around the room. Her eyes landed on my Vota Communista! poster, taken from a lamppost in Pisa. She chuckled, nodded, chuckled again. I know this act. I expected her to tell me that she was once a bohemian too, in college.

"So far, Mr. Blackburn, you haven't told me anything I don't already know."

"I'd like to cooperate. But I don't know what you want."

"We'd like to speak to Hart Denby. But we're not sure where he is."

"He runs a school for poets down there."

"We know that. He left his school days ago. Do you know about the antique scams?"

I decided to play dumb. Or maybe I wasn't playing. "Antiques?"

"Seems Hart, and possibly his sister, were fencing various stolen items."

"Is that a federal offense?"

"Why are you so interested in jurisdictional matters? Illegal monies were moved from state to state. Also stolen goods. Satisfied?"

"I guess I'm surprised that you guys would bother."

"We can pretty much do what we want, you know. Some of the stolen items were owned by the rich and the powerful. Somebody donates to a campaign, somebody gets robbed, somebody says, Congressman, put your best on this one."

"I'm not sure how I can help you."

"Look, this is a dumb case. We've got more important things to do. We need a patsy. We don't really need a conviction, just an arrest. I could find a way to stick you with it. After all, you did just kill Stephanie Hearn. You're in real trouble! If we come in and find one little antique, say an earring, or a brooch, you're the fall guy. But if I can get to Hart, I may be able to recover some of the loot. Mr. Rich Donor would love that."

I sat, silent. The ways of law enforcement are far over my head. Agent Dao sat on my bed, looking smug. The phone rang.

"Aren't you going to get that?"

"It's OK. I've got voicemail."

"I'm going to want to wrap this up in a couple of days. And I'm going to make it easy on you. Just a good solid lead. I want to find Hart."

"What if he's still in Mexico?""

"It doesn't matter. We have connections down there."

"I don't know where he is."

"You see what you can do. Like I said, a good solid

lead. You do that for us and you won't be charged with murder."

"Just like that?"

She looked me straight in the eye. It was the sincere look of a really good politician. Agent Dao was on her way up the ladder. She'd be Attorney General someday. "I can guess what happened, Mr. Blackburn. Stephie had a reputation before this came up. She probably had you wrapped around her little finger. And you did something she didn't like and she went off. Right?"

"Yes."

"You're not the first. You just got lucky."

"Lucky?"

"Lucky you weren't standing next to the window." Agent Dao stood up and went over to my desk. Wrote a number on the back of her card. "You call this number, you say it's a message for me, and you leave the information on the voice mail. I'll regard it as an anonymous tip. You wait three, four days. If you don't get booked for murder you can consider it my doing. I'm sure your lead will be good. I hear you do a little detective work on the side."

She shook my hand. Before she left she pointed at the pipe and chuckled. Said, "You should be more careful!"

The phone message was from Dean Centro. Check your email! I went down to Moe's to use the public e-mail machine. I got grave, embarrassed hellos from the clerks. They'd obviously heard about Stephie's fall. I logged on to my dummy account, which was probably being monitored by the FBI. I wondered if they'd let me have the loot from Oriana, or if they'd set me up. I decided to go through the motions. What else could I do? My life was in the hands of the corporate dictatorship. As always. But today was a big reminder of that fact.

The e-mail said, "Roma, Friday morning coffee. Find a noisy table." I had two days to wait.

27.

Marvin came over, straight from a "business trip" to the Balkans. He asked me not to ask about it, so I didn't. Somehow he'd already heard about Stephie. It didn't even occur to me to ask how. He arrived with a grocery bag full of goodies. He decided that I needed a long heavy dinner with lots to drink.

Marvin's not a great cook, but he has a few good recipes. And he buys great ingredients. He made a risotto with a very rich stock, bought at some gourmet store. It tasted as if they'd stewed a dozen chickens and a bushel of onions in premium white wine for six months. Said risotto was fortified with gorgonzola and prosciutto. This was served with a heavy Barolo, the kind of red wine that you can chew. With our second bottle of Barolo we had thick veal chops and kale with balsamic vinegar. After dinner he produced a tall, skinny bottle of grappa. I recognized the label. He'd bought it in Naples a few years back. This was possibly his last bottle. I told my long sad story, finishing about halfway through my chop. He lifted his glass and toasted me, referring to our victory dinner. I took offense.

"C'mon Marvin. It was self defense, I know. I can live with it. But it wasn't a blow for international socialism. Actually, it was kind of tawdry."

"Bullshit. One less SUV, one less dotcommer. You said yourself that she admitted to being a killer. She wasn't killing fascists. She had it coming. The world is a little cleaner now."

I couldn't accept that, but I was too beat to argue. I shifted subjects. "How do I get out of this one, Marv?"

"Simple. Weldon and Trak. Give 'em to the FBI. They'll talk."

"Aren't they out of the country, too?"

"Trak's been hanging around Santa Cruz. Don't ask me how I know. Haven't heard about Weldon. Trak should be enough."

"Trak once told me that Weldon killed Peggy."

"And maybe he did. But right now you need to get Bailey Dao off your tail. You just lead Agent Dao to Trak, and he'll talk. He probably knows. I assume he's up here tying up loose ends for Hart. Then it's off to Uraguay, or Panama, or some other place where you can change your name and live like a king off the sale of a few antiques."

"He'll have to give up the poetry fantasy camp."

"That was probably a scam, too. Get some big names, pay them a deposit up front. Get full payment out of the students. Disappear."

"Creeley will be pretty pissed. I wouldn't want to be on his bad side."

And we both chuckled at the thought of a pissed-off Robert Creeley.

28.

I woke up early. A late summer heat wave had hit the Bay Area. I put on jeans and a T-shirt, then switched to a white dress shirt. Wanted to look good for old Dino. I went to a rental place on Oxford. I rented another Neon, a green bubble with a scooter-sized engine. I drove over to College Avenue and circled for parking. Got lucky and found a space across the street from Roma.

Dino knew from our sleepovers that I take my first dose of coffee at 8:30. I found a noisy table in the middle of the front room, in front of the espresso line. People in various work uniforms were ordering their coffee to go, fuel for the walk to the BART station. I felt sorry for them. And they were the lucky ones! The average commuter's day starts at about 6:30. I dumped sugar in my single espresso, in a real cup, not a paper one with a lid. People who drink their coffee Seattle style simply lack class. Can't trust 'em. I gave my coffee a slow stir with my cute little spoon. I moved my chair so that I could better see the door. No Dino.

Baldwin Mrabet approached my table. He's a retired teacher. In the fifties he was blacklisted, although racism probably would have kept him out of academia anyway. During the wars of the sixties he shot a cop in Oakland. I know this for a fact, although he never got caught. Miraculously, he wasn't framed or chased out of the country like most of his friends. He moved in with his mother in St. Louis until things cooled off. In the late seventies he emerged as a memoirist. Affirmative action helped him get a job as a lecturer at Hayward State. Now retired, he's nearing eighty. I'm usually happy to see him, but I had other things on my mind.

"You look nervous, Holmes."

"I think I'm in the process of being stood up."

"Man or a woman?"

"Guy."

"I won't ask."

"But you'd like to."

"No, no. Gossip doesn't interest me that much. I'm going to join you because all the other tables are full. If your date comes, I'll leave."

He had a normal cup of coffee in a mug. He sat down, and as he leaned foreward, into his drink, he winced.

"Back problem?"

"I took a good shot in the ribs during one of my, um, adventures. Never healed. This was years ago."

"Sounds like a story."

"Won't bore you with it now. Except to say this. We were tough!"

I'd heard this before, but I liked it. I nodded respectfully and waited for more.

"In the forties and fifties, if you were a red, your heroes were Hemingway, Sarte, Debs, Paul Robeson. Those guys kicked ass. We never backed away from a bar fight. And the women! Emma Goldman was the prototype. She could have kicked both of our butts, right into her seventies. Even in the sixties there was Angela Davis, and a few like her that you've never heard of. Who do girls look up to now? Oprah Winfrey? Alice Walker? Martha Stewart? Shit. I see these kids in Philly and Seattle, and they just lie down. They got to learn how to shoot to kill."

The espresso hit me as he finished his little speech. I felt awake and alive, and happy to be in Berkeley. Baldwin downed his coffee, shook my hand, and strode out of the café on the legs of a younger man.

Still no Dino.

I got myself another, this time decaf. I didn't want to be too jittery. Lots to do today. I sat back down at the same table and dosed my coffee with sugar. Then, at last, Dino Centro. Looking very nervous.

He gave me a broad, phony smile and shook my hand. Didn't sit down. He leaned over and spoke softly. "Let's pretend it's a chance meeting. I can feel the heat closing in."

"I know, Dino. They're out there making their moves. It's my fault."

"What should we do?"

"We'll just do what we do and hope that they don't care too much. I think they're looking for bigger fish. Sit down. And don't lose it. It'll only make things worse. They may think we're hiding more than we are."

He took off his seersucker jacket and sat down. Maybe, some warm day, I will find the courage that it takes to wear seersucker. Dino carried it off beautifully.

"Do you want me to just sit here and talk about it?"

"Sure, why not?" Over Dino's shoulder I could see one of Bailey Dao's boys in the espresso line. Young, good-looking, crewcut, clothes too obviously casual. A little too bemused by all the characters. I silenced Dino by putting a finger on my lips. Mr. Agent got his coffee and found a table, out of earshot.

"It's OK now. What's up?"

"I made the sale and I have your cut. And I want to get the cash out of my place. His eyes got bright, then narrowed into that silly Latin lover look. "Clay, I hope we'll have some time to say a proper goodbye, but if we don't, I want to tell you that it was great. Perhaps our paths will cross again."

I met his gaze with my own smoky look. I wondered if it was as comical. "You're a great lay, dear Dino. And I like you a lot. I hope we do meet again. Now, where's that money!"

"Still at my place."

"Leaving it there was a risk."

"Stupid of me. I'm too nervous to think. I'm in over my head. I just want to get this over with and go to Buenos Aires. Will you come see me? We could take tango lessons."

"I'll be happy to. If The Man lets us pull this off."

"I don't know what I'm doing. You do the thinking for both of us."

"I intend to. Just follow me to my rental car."

We drove to Dino's, a couple of miles down College Ave. Found parking close by. A good omen. We went up to his little studio. I went over to the window. Down below in the BART parking lot Efram Zimbalist Jr. was leaning on the hood of his black Buick. Raybans, dress shoes, head big and square. Storm trooper. I waved, but he didn't acknowledge me. No sense of humor.

Dino went into his closet and dug around. Came out with a gym bag. Pulled out a T-shirt and some shorts. Dumped the money on the bed. It made an impressive pile. He produced a piece of legal sized paper. It was a list of his expenses. I accepted them with a nod. I took it for granted that they were hinky. A bite here, a bite there. My personal expenses come to about $22,000 a year. There was enough to last about four years. Okay by me.

"Do you want to count it?"

"I'm going to trust you, Dino." I repacked the gym bag.

"So this is goodbye."

"Until I decide to take tango lessons."

"He hung his head. You'll never come."

"Life is long, Dino. We'll meet again."

"Hope so." This time his look was sincere. Or at least convincing.

I walked him over to the window. He didn't like that idea at first, but he loosened up when I kissed him. He tried to waltz me back to the bed, but I knew what I wanted. I pushed him back to the window. Over his shoulder I could see Agent Square Head. It was a nice big double window, almost ceiling to almost floor. Dino leaned against the partition that separated the panes as I kissed him again. I unzipped his tight Euro jeans. He flopped out, half hard. I stroked the shaft with my slightly sweaty palm. Success. I slid down to my knees and I blew him like a symphony. I stood up, knees a little wobbly. I stepped to the left and looked out the window at the agent. Opened my mouth and stuck my tongue out, to prove that I'd swallowed. He looked away.

I positioned myself so that the shithead could see all of me in profile. "Hey, Dino Centro, it's my turn."

"Right there? Clay, you're a very kinky man."

Dino was very, very good. Hmm. Tango lessons. He finished, then he kissed me. The taste of my come on his tongue. Nothing like it.

Shithead shifted around, then got in the car. Sex is politics, fucker. I flipped him off as he drove away.

"Who was that for?"

"Somebody was watching us."

"You don't say! A pervert!"

One last laugh, and one more kiss, and we were on our way.

29.

I threw the loot in the trunk of the car and headed for the freeway. Down 880 to the dreaded Highway 17, the quickest way to Santa Cruz. The Neon did OK over the mountain road. But I still missed the Miata. I probably wouldn't bother to buy another one. I'd use my insurance money to get an older Japanese pickup. Better for scouting books.

There was no sign of the black Buick as I entered downtown Santa Cruz. I had lunch at a Chinese noodle place on the Pacific Garden Mall. I expected to see my agent voyeur, but he didn't show. I downed a Tsingtao to steel my nerves for the final detail.

I parked the Neon in downtown Felton. Took the strigil out of the glove compartment and put it in a canvas book bag. I had saved it to have as a souvenir. Now I would put it to good use. I walked up the deserted streets to Trak's house. Better to do this mid-day, when all the techies would be at their jobs in Silicon Valley. If Trak was home I'd go back to Santa Cruz, find a hotel, and try again late at night.

There was no car in the garage. I went around to the

back. All I had to do was place the strigil in a semi-obvious hiding place. Call Bailey Dao and make my anonymous tip.

There was some shrubbery. Who would put it there? Under the mattress of the chaise lounge? That wouldn't work either. I decided to go into the house. I got in through an open bathroom window. There was a nice old desk in one of the bedrooms. Another stolen antique? I hid the strigel under some papers just as I heard a car pull into the drive. I decided, too late, that breaking into the house was a stupid thing to do. Or maybe the old subconscious wanted me to be there. Can't resist fucking with a yuppie.

As he came in the door I hit him with a good straight shot to the side of the face. My hand would be swollen for days. He went down, then he started to get up. I kicked him hard in the same place. He was out for awhile. I looked around the house. He had one of those clawfoot bathtubs. I dragged him into the bathroom. He started to come to so I kicked him again, harder. I went into the laundry room and found some rope and some rags. I tied one leg to the clawfoot tub, tied his hands together, and gagged him. He had a cell phone on his belt. I picked it up, dropped it, and stepped on it. On the way out I grabbed his home phone and took it with me. Smashed it on the front porch.

As I left I realized that my fingerprints were everywhere. Then I laughed. If the cops wanted me they could have me. The FBI would either protect me or hand me over. It was all up to Bailey Dao.

I decided to take Highway 1 back home. A little slower, but the coast would calm my nerves. I stopped at a Safeway on the north side of Santa Cruz. I found a pay phone and called the number on Dao's card.

"Bailey Dao."

"I thought this was your voicemail?"

"I just happened to be by the phone."

"It's Clay."

"I know. Let's pretend I don't."

"How do I know I can trust you?"

"Doesn't matter. Somebody saw the whole thing."

"I didn't notice."

"He's pretty good."

"Did he change cars?"

"Agent Lovelace handed things off to somebody in the Santa Cruz office. He didn't like your little performance."

"Just having a little fun."

"Dangerous fun. But you got us what we need, so I'll go along with the deal. You did get us a lead. Right?"

"There's a strigil in Trak's desk. It's probably stolen."

"A what?"

"Look it up. You can use it as a bargaining chip. Tell Trak you'll send him up for grand theft, strigil if he doesn't lead you to Hart. He knows where Hart is. I don't know if you're interested, but you might also ask him about Peggy Denby. I think they killed her."

"We might get around to that at some point."

"How do I know if I can trust you?"

"Don't worry. The fix is in. You won't be bothered. Enjoy the money."

"You can let me go, just like that? Hart must have really gotten into something big."

"Stay out of it. And don't talk about this. We can still arrest you if we feel like it. We do pretty much what we want."

30.

Roasting a chicken should be easy but it isn't. Little things matter. The chicken has to be thoroughly dried after washing. Then I pull up the skin of the breast and fill it with herbs and garlic. I like to stuff it with quartered oranges and onions. Keeps it from drying out. I have a great roasting pan that I got at Sur La Table. Cost me a week's pay, but worth it. I like to roast root vegetables in the same pan. Parsnip is good, and yams. And of course potatoes. A couple of different types, if possible. The oven has to be preheated to high heat. I drop the heat when I put the chicken in the oven.

Marvin arrived as the bird was beginning to brown. He pulled two bottles of Tavel from his book bag. Tavel is a wonderful pink wine. They drink it like water in France, but it doesn't get exported. They keep it for themselves.

"Where'd you get those? Is Alice Notley in town?"

"I spent two days in Paris. Just got off the plane."

"Marvin! When are you going to start telling me about your international adventures?"

"You may well be ready to hear about them, m'boy."

But he only told me what he ate for dinner, and what poets he ran into. The first night he had couscous with William Talcott and Jim Nisbet. Lunched with Summer

Brenner on the second day.

"For poor folk, poets sure do get around."

"And now you can afford to, too. What are we going to do with that loot?"

"We?"

Sly smile. We both knew I owed him something for his help on the, uh, case.

"Any suggestions?"

"I have some work to do, south of the border. How about if we fly down to La Paz and swim in the Sea of Cortez."

"I was 86'd from La Paz, remember?"

"I can fix that. All we have to do is take a little side trip to Chiapas."

"Sounds mysterious."

"It is. But I'm ready to let you in on some of my little secrets."

"As far as I know they haven't picked up Hart. He could still be down there."

"If he is we'll beat the holy shit out of him and leave his bones in the desert. You're a rich man now, Clay. We could bribe the authorities, and the world would be none the wiser."

"And what of Weldon?"

"For all we know he's at the bottom of the San Francisco Bay. But if he turns up down there, we'll kill him too."

"Maybe we can get Robert Creeley to pay us some bounty."

"Creeley can do it himself. He's tougher than the both of us. And, from all accounts he's armed to the teeth."

We finished the chicken and both bottles, then he went back to his bag and returned with some very good armangac. We discussed our future trip. We changed destinations a couple of times, from Mexico to Thailand to North Africa. But Marvin kept steering me toward La Paz. At morning's light we shook on it. I took a nap, called a cat sitter and packed my bag. Onward to the Sea of Cortez.

Photo by Liz Leger

Owen Hill is the author of six books of poetry and a collection of stories, *Loose Ends* (Thumbscrew Press, San Francisco). He lives in Berkeley, California.